Elizabeth's heart sped up, pounding in her chest.

She hated herself at that moment for the instant reaction she always had to a strange man's interest—fear. And this time it was worse. It all but swamped her. It was so much worse than usual, she had a hard time hiding her reaction. Reaching inside herself for the courage she drew on to get through difficult times, Elizabeth forced herself to hold her ground and smile rather than back away and flee.

"Ms. Boyer, pleased to make your acquaintance," Jack Alton said, as if abruptly aware that staring was rude. Then he dipped his head in a polite, cowboylike salute that went perfectly with his Western accent.

"And it's a pleasure to meet you, as well," she said, not meaning a word of it. She hated that interest she saw in his eyes. Almost hated him for having it…

Books by Kate Welsh

Love Inspired

For the Sake of Her Child #39
Never Lie to an Angel #69
A Family for Christmas #83
Small-Town Dreams #100
Their Forever Love #120
*The Girl Next Door #156
*Silver Lining #173
*Mountain Laurel #187
*Her Perfect Match #196

*Laurel Glen

KATE WELSH

is a two-time winner of Romance Writers of America's coveted Golden Heart award and a finalist for RWA's RITA® Award in 1999. Kate lives in Havertown, Pennsylvania, with her husband of over thirty years. When not at work in her home office, creating stories and the characters that populate them, Kate fills her time in other creative outlets. There are few crafts she hasn't tried at least once or a sewing project that hasn't been a delicious temptation. Those ideas she can't resist grace her home or those of friends and family.

As a child she often lost herself in creating make-believe worlds and happily-ever-after tales. Kate turned back to creating happy endings when her husband challenged her to write down the stories in her head. With Jesus so much a part of her life, Kate found it natural to incorporate Him in her writing. Her goal is to entertain her readers with wholesome stories of the love between two people the Lord has brought together and to teach His truth while she entertains.

HER PERFECT MATCH

KATE WELSH

Published by Steeple Hill Books™

STEEPLE HILL BOOKS

ISBN 0-373-87203-8

HER PERFECT MATCH

Visit us at www.steeplehill.com

Printed in U.S.A.

Therefore, if anyone is in Christ, he is a new creation; old things have passed away; behold, all things have become new.

—*II Corinthians* 5:17

To Patience Smith.

This one's for you.
Thanks for all the encouragement and
guidance in my career.
And thanks also for Elizabeth.
You are an inspiration.

Prologue

"Then who am I?" Jackson Alton's broken whisper was nearly inaudible against the backdrop of the Colorado blizzard raging outside the cabin windows.

Such a simple question, he thought. Any thirty-two-year-old man should know the answer. Minutes ago he'd thought he did. But that was before.

Jackson stared at the adoption papers in his hand, a hard knot having formed in his chest. A split second's decision—whether to sort through a box of papers or put them in the musty ranch house attic untouched—had not only changed his perception of the life he'd led so far and had planned to lead in the future. It had altered something more essential. It had shifted his vision of who he was.

He sat alone on the floor of his mother's studio—the shrine his father has kept to his late wife for twenty-eight years. He stopped his thoughts right there and demanded of himself what no one had the guts to say before. Not his mother. Not his father.

Jackson looked around the small cabin he'd planned to move into any day now. He'd decided he needed a little personal space, and Evan Alton had finally reconciled himself to the idea that it was time to clear out his wife's studio. Now Jackson felt he no longer belonged there. But then where *did* he belong?

He hadn't a clue.

And the really scary thing was Jackson might never have known the truth if he hadn't volunteered to clear out the cabin. He'd been afraid Evan might slide into a depression if he had to go through his wife's things.

He clenched his fist, wrinkling the papers in his hand. In a moment of clarity, he realized that the depth of his anger at this revelation he'd stumbled across was really mostly caused by his father's on-going deep preoccupation with the loss of his wife— even to the detriment of his children.

Though Evan had been a positive presence in their lives, Jackson had always instinctively known that something a parent should have given hadn't been given to him. And he'd missed it.

With the March blizzard howling outside, Jackson once again stared at the piece of paper he'd unconsciously wadded into a ball. He turned it over and over examining twists and turns of something that, like his life, had been smooth and neat only moments before. He shook his head and smoothed out the crumpled ball before leafing through the rest of the documents and notes in the box on his lap.

The papers with the official adoption decree answered several of his questions. His father's name was Lieutenant Wade Jackson, which must be why his name was Jackson Wade. His mother was a Broadway actress named Margaret Taggert—she used Meg as a stage name. There was a Broadway playbill from *Hello, Dolly!* in the late sixties. Her name was circled. She'd been in the chorus. There was a sort of family tree on the Taggerts in a handwriting completely foreign to him. He found himself hoping it was his mother's hand—that she'd cared enough to personally record the information so she'd be sure he had it.

The Taggert family—his family—lived in Pennsylvania on a horse farm called Laurel Glen. How weird was that? Maybe not very, he realized. Meg Taggert might have sought out a life for her son parallel to the one she'd had growing up. After all, the Circle A was a ranch with horses, though they raised cattle as their main livelihood. His horse breeding program was his sideline.

There was nothing about his father other than his name, however. He sorted through the rest of box, hoping to find something to tie him to the mysterious Wade Jackson other than being named after him. At the bottom of the box he found a tiny manila envelope. He opened the flap and turned it over in his palm. A sparkling diamond ring fell into his hand.

"I guess they were engaged and something went wrong," he muttered, examining the initials inscribed on the inside.

Wade Jackson had been listed with a title. Lieutenant. The Vietnam War had still been going on about then. He might have been killed, but wouldn't that have given Meg Taggert more of a reason to keep Wade Jackson's child? Logic told him his father must have been killed, because if Meg Taggert's relationship with Jackson had ended bitterly, she wouldn't have requested his child be named after him and she wouldn't have left the ring for that child.

Something suddenly occurred to him that wasn't completely unrelated. He wondered if his sister, Crystal, was adopted, too. He glanced at the picture of Martha Alton and her mother—the grandmother who'd raised him. No way was Crystal adopted. She was the spitting image of the woman who had been his mother for four years. Crystal had the same Native American cheekbones and onyx eyes that stared at him from the thirty-year-old picture. He, on the other hand, looked nothing like anyone else in the family. Apparently he'd just found out why. It had never bothered him before—that different face from all the rest. It did now, and he hated that it did.

"Why would he not tell me? Why the secrecy?" Jackson asked the silent room. It didn't escape his notice that whenever he had deep personal questions, he usually talked to God, but this time he found himself unable or unwilling to turn to Him. Instead, Jackson talked to an empty room.

Feeling every bit as empty, Jackson stood and gathered all the papers, unsuccessfully fighting anger. He didn't need God to answer his questions. Evan Alton had the answers and had kept them to himself for thirty-two years. And Jackson wanted those answers. Now!

Chapter One

Elizabeth Boyer was not a happy camper. She was on her way from Boyerton, her parents' estate, to make apologies to her best friend's family in her father's name. She felt it was her duty and the right thing to do even though it wasn't her responsibility. Typical of Reginald Boyer's self-centered way of thinking, he felt he'd done nothing wrong.

Her heart heavy, she drove toward the private road through Laurel Glen with its iron archway at the entrance that had made the horse farm a Chester County landmark. The mountain laurel that lined the drive was already in full bloom on that second day of July. It was a scene fit for a postcard.

Or at least it would have been if there weren't TV news vans and various other cars clustered about the entrance like vultures hoping for a tasty set of bones to pick. As she rounded the bend right before the drive and flipped on her turn signal, she saw them.

They turned as one toward her car, and all of them seemed to focus on her tattletale blinker.

It was too late to drive on by. And unfortunately, because it was a cool day, she'd driven from the car wash with the windows down. So within a split second of realizing the inevitability of a confrontation with the reporters, Elizabeth had three microphones jammed in her face and three nearly identical camera eyes peered at her.

"What is your business here? Are you a federal inspector? Are you an employee?" The run-on question came from three separate voices, but they were all of one mind.

Elizabeth thought instantly of her father and the statement he'd given the press. It was the reason she was there and had been a self-serving attempt to divert attention off his culpability in the current crisis at Laurel Glen. But then again, there had been polite bad blood between Reginald Boyer and Ross Taggert, owner of Laurel Glen, for years, and this was just another volley in an undeclared war that was mostly in her father's mind.

She decided to give the reporters a statement, hoping to balance her father's criticism of her friend Cole Taggert for trying to save the mare that had come down with West Nile Virus.

"My name is Elizabeth Boyer," she said. "The infected mosquitoes were breeding in my parents' unopened pool."

That caused an excited murmur to move through the crowd of journalists behind the news crews. They took to scribbling in their notebooks at the speed of light.

"According to your father he doesn't feel at all responsible. He sees this as a natural occurrence. Do you agree?"

"I believe the animal comes from an area of the country where this isn't a problem and the vaccine is still in short supply. I think everyone should be mindful that standing water can promote mosquitoes and that we have a dangerous strain of encephalitis moving into the area. I've been told that simple precautions are very effective against this sort of natural occurrence."

"Do you agree with your father's bleak assessment of the Laurel Glen mare's chance for survival?" another of the three microphone-toting reporters asked.

"No. I most certainly do not agree. Dr. Taggert would never do anything detrimental or cruel to an animal. He decided to treat her rather than euthanize her, and she happens to be on the mend. That's all I have to say. Kindly clear the road," she demanded, using the imperious tone she'd heard her mother use time and again to intimidate others into doing her bidding without question. It worked now, as it always did.

Minutes later, after waving to the farmworker who'd moved the makeshift barricade from across the road, Elizabeth glanced into her rearview mirror at the clustered news vans and reporters. She couldn't shake the vision of vultures from her mind.

She found Laurel Glen relatively quiet, unlike what

she'd heard it had been like for the last several days with investigators crawling everywhere. They'd been trying without success to find the source of the West Nile Virus that had infected a mare belonging to Laurel Glen's female trainer. That was because Elizabeth's parents' pool had never been opened, and the source of the infection was the water in the winter pool cover.

Elizabeth parked in the small lot behind the first two of four stone and brick stables that formed an X with a large competition-size practice ring connecting them. She stepped into the unusual cool of the sunny, breezy July day and headed toward the clinic. As she walked next to the practice ring, she was surprised to see Cole Taggert bent over the engine of one of the big tractors used to mow the hay.

Cole was the least mechanical person she'd ever met.

"I hope this means CJ's mare is even better today," she said, stepping next to him. "But I've got to wonder if success hasn't gone your head. Unless something drastic has happened in the last several days you're not exactly qualified to operate on a tractor, Dr. Taggert."

She sucked in a quick breath and stepped back when he stood straight and looked at her with eyes the color of the night sky. It wasn't Cole at all but Jack Alton, the new foreman. She remembered in a flash the dinner at Laurel Glen last week when she'd met him the first time. She'd made the same mistake then....

* * *

As she'd crossed the threshold of Laurel House's parlor, Ross Taggert laughed at something his son, Cole, had said. Elizabeth was surprised because the two of them usually reacted to each other like gasoline and a lit match. She was about to loop an arm around Cole's waist and join them—she was, in fact, only a couple feet from doing just that—when she stopped in her tracks.

Cole was across the room! She watched him engage in an earnest discussion with CJ Larson, Laurel Glen's trainer. She blinked, doubting her sanity as well as her eyes, then she turned to Ross Taggert and the Cole Taggert look-alike.

"And this lovely lady is—" Ross was speaking as she studied the two men near her "—Elizabeth Boyer, Cole's, ah, friend. Elizabeth, I'd like you to meet our new foreman, Jack Alton."

Jack Alton's deep, nearly indigo eyes startled her almost as much as his resemblance to Cole did. Elizabeth searched his features, looking at both the striking resemblance and the small nuances of difference. His hair, though close in color to Cole's, was definitely a shade darker, making it nearly black. His cheekbones were a bit sharper, his jaw a bit more chiseled. He was taller, too, though only by an inch or two. But it was those eyes, Taggert blue, Cole's aunt Meg called them, which Cole did not have, that took her breath away when he leveled them on her. The new foreman and Cole could be brothers, but standing next to him felt nothing like the safe feeling being near Cole gave her. Jack Alton stared at her openly for a long uncomfortable moment. The look in those blue, blue eyes of his was nothing like the brotherly expression Cole had when he looked at her, either.

Elizabeth's heart sped up, pounding in her chest. She hated herself at that moment for the instant reaction she always had to a strange man's interest— fear. And this time it was worse. It all but swamped her. It was so much worse than usual it was hard to hide her reaction. Reaching inside herself for the courage she drew on to get through difficult times, Elizabeth forced herself to hold her ground and smile rather than back away and flee.

"Ms. Boyer, pleased to make your acquaintance," Jack Alton said, as if abruptly aware that staring was rude. Then he dipped his head in a polite cowboy-like salute that went perfectly with his western accent.

"And it's a pleasure to meet you, as well," she said, not meaning a word of it. She hated that interest she saw in his eyes. Hated him for having it....

And being near him was just as bad this time. Her heart pounded so loudly she could hardly hear over its thunder, and she felt light-headed and breathless, too.

"Sorry to disappoint you, Ms. Boyer," Jack Alton said a little disdainfully. "Cole's been tied up these last few days. Seems *someone* let their pool become a mosquito breeding ground and it's caused a lot of trouble around here. I hope you haven't brought any more infection with you."

He had that same look in his eyes he'd had the other night, but today there was anger, too, and there was no one around to deflect the male intensity of his gaze. She took another step back. Unsettled, she resorted to haughtiness, as she always did to cover her anxiety. She knew it didn't win her friends but she didn't care. It was yet another lesson she'd learned from her mother and one of the few she agreed with. Finding yourself disliked was better than having your weaknesses exposed to the world.

"I'm well aware of the problems and the cause," she told him, working to interweave every word with icy disdain. "I took precautions. And I'll express my apologies where they're due. I don't need hints from you as to my duties and you, sir, are due no apology. You are *paid* for the time you put in at Laurel Glen."

She'd apologized to Cole for the problems and for her father's outrageous statement to the press. She couldn't imagine how Reginald could have told the world Cole was wasting resources on an animal that should be put down.

Elizabeth turned and started toward the barn, but Jack Alton stepped in her path. Again, she backed away from him. "What?" she demanded, reaching for anger to drown her uneasiness.

"Cole doesn't need any more pressure to put that mare down."

Her temper notched up. Anger felt better than fear. She gave him an icy glare. "Mr. Alton, just because my father says something, that doesn't mean I automatically adopt it as gospel. Morning is a beautiful creature and, from what I understand, she's the only thing CJ has left from her life with her parents, who are deceased. Knowing Cole as I do, I'd expect nothing less from him than desperate measures to save his patient. And I applaud those efforts. Now if you will kindly get out of my way, I'd like to go see for myself how well Morning is doing today.''

Jack Alton stepped smartly to the side and bowed. ''Yes, your highness. Anything you say, your highness.''

Tempted for some odd reason to smile, she waved a dismissive hand the way the royal Elizabeth might. ''It is so much more pleasant when the peasants know their place,'' she quipped in her haughtiest tone. Then, as if she hadn't a care in the world, Elizabeth sailed off toward Laurel Glen's historic barn and the clinic Cole had recently modernized.

Her stomach churned as she pretended not to hear Jack Alton's deep rumbling laughter following her. Elizabeth was acutely disturbed that she'd let him frighten her so badly when he'd stepped in her path, especially since she was sure he hadn't meant to be at all threatening. She had to think it was due to his strange resemblance to the Taggert family and his unexplained presence. She feared they had a wolf in sheep's clothing in their midst.

But even with a plausible excuse, she still hated the fear that had taken her unaware and hated herself for feeling it. Her one small consolation was that no one knew what a coward she was inside, where her fear of men was a living thing clawing at her and threatening to show itself to the world at any time.

Elizabeth entered the barn. The old building had been converted into offices, rest rooms and an animal clinic years ago. She walked down the hall toward the clinic and heard Cole's sister Hope's voice raised in anger. Choosing not to retreat in case Cole needed her support, she forged ahead and arrived to hear Hope Carrington, who lived on the neighboring property, scolding him because he'd kissed CJ Larson then had discounted it as meaningless. Their backs were toward her, so neither knew she was there.

"Obviously a kiss means a lot more to her than you," Hope chastised her brother. "Really, Cole, how could you toy with someone as inexperienced as CJ Larson? She isn't in Elizabeth's league, and you know it!"

"And how, Hope dear, would you know what *league* I'm in?" Elizabeth demanded, hoping to draw Hope's fire. She owed that to Cole and so much more. Elizabeth refused to be cowed by his sister's disapproval. Instead she walked to stand next to him, crossing her arms and looking imperiously down her nose at Cole's younger sister.

"Play in the mud, Elizabeth, and you get it all over yourself," Hope said, glaring. "It's really quite easy to spot," she continued, then she looked at Cole with fire in her blue eyes. "I'll go see if I can calm CJ down."

"Leave CJ alone!" Cole snapped. Elizabeth zoned out on the rest of the argument. Her thoughts turned inward. Why, when she'd been no more than a casual date for any man, did Hope and others around Laurel Glen see through her mask to her soiled soul? Elizabeth had successfully hidden her secret shame from society at large for going on fifteen years, but it didn't seem to stay hidden at Laurel Glen.

"Save the world from obnoxious little sisters," Cole grumbled as Hope stalked out.

"Mind telling me what I did to get on Hope's wrong side? *Again?*" Elizabeth asked.

"It's my fault," Cole admitted. "And I'm sorry. I've been using you and I just did it again. Not only didn't I ask you for permission first but now I have to ask you to continue the charade."

"Used me how, and what charade?"

Cole grimaced. "My family just assumes we're, well, you know—*involved*. And I've just let them go on assuming."

Stunned, Elizabeth dropped into the chair next to him. Betrayal from Cole was something she wasn't prepared to deal with. He was her best friend. Her only real friend. The only person in the world she'd thought she could trust. "Oh, Cole, how could you? I trusted you."

She couldn't ever remember not trusting Cole. Not since he'd appeared out of nowhere like an avenging angel the day Jason Lexington had lured her into the woods behind the high school. Cole had dragged her attacker to his feet and beaten the older, much larger senior until he'd run him off. Then the natural-born healer in Cole had replaced the tough-guy image he'd always projected at school. He'd calmed her, taken care of her, told her sweet lies about how she was just the same as she'd always been. Then he'd taken her home where he'd foolishly thought she would be cared for by her parents.

Had he not seen her running along the road later that night and stopped her, she might have done something foolish and changed her life forever. She'd gone out that night looking for trouble, hoping to publicly embarrass her parents with a deliberate act since they were embarrassed by one she'd had no control over. Somehow Cole had convinced her that she was only hurting herself.

"I *am* your friend," Cole said now. "Have I ever told a single soul you were with me that night I stole the police car? Have I even admitted anyone was with me? I just didn't see any harm in not continuing to deny a relationship when they wouldn't believe me anyway."

"But that's probably why they don't approve of me."

"You don't know that. Just because they're married doesn't mean Hope's forgiven you. You have to see that she's still jealous because she thinks you and Jeff were involved. It's why they all assume we are. I don't think anyone but you, me and Jeff believes you've only been friends to the two of us. And my aunt Meg actually likes you a lot. She just doesn't think we suit each other, and we've both agreed that's true. Right? You do still feel only friendship toward me?"

She noted the panic in his brown eyes. "Don't get that worried look. You aren't about to break my heart." Then an idea occurred to her. "Oh. But you *have* broken that nice CJ Larson's heart and you used me as an excuse to do it. Am I right?"

Cole gave her a soulful look. "I didn't mean to."

She wasn't buying the innocent act for a second. "Oh? Did someone else put the words in your mouth? A fairy snuck in here and cast a spell on you?"

She was satisfied with the color that invaded his cheeks. He explained that he'd been trying to discourage CJ because he was a disaster with relationships and didn't want to hurt the pretty trainer even worse later on. Cole was basically a nice guy with issues of his own to deal with. So Elizabeth decided to let him use her as a smoke screen until he had himself straightened out, though she felt she needed to attach a condition.

"Okay, but you have to get your family to believe I've never been more than a friend. Your father practically choked trying to describe our relationship to Jack Alton at dinner the other night. Now I know why 'friend' was so hard for him to say."

"I'm sorry. I'll do what I can as soon as I can."

Elizabeth nodded. "Now about Jack Alton," she said, taking the opportunity to change the subject. She was really bothered by the new Laurel Glen hire. Were they all wearing blinders? After the trouble with their former foreman, who was in prison for murder and several counts of attempted murder perpetrated at Laurel Glen, it boggled her mind that no one was questioning Jack Alton's suspicious resemblance to the entire Taggert family. She had to believe her extreme reactions to him were a signal that he was up to some sort of mischief. "Tell me about your new foreman," she demanded.

Cole nodded as if on her wavelength. "Jack Alton. Spooky, huh? Dad and Amelia seem to think it's coincidence. I think as good an influence as Amelia has been on Dad since they met and got married, she should have left a little of his cynicism intact. At least Hope and Jeff are suspicious."

"What do you know about him?"

"He's from Colorado, not far from Greeley. He attended the University of Northern Colorado there. Grew up on a ranch called the Circle A. He's not getting along with his father so he decided to strike out on his own. His personal and business references checked out."

"But what's he doing here?" she asked. The resemblance was just too coincidental.

Cole shook his head, looking worried. "Good question."

Chapter Two

Jackson Wade Alton—Jack to everyone at Laurel Glen and Jackson to everyone on the Circle A back home in Colorado—watched from the darkened doorway of Stable Four as Elizabeth Boyer climbed into her little sports car and drove off. The woman had haunted his thoughts from the moment he'd laid eyes on her at dinner the other night.

Actually it had started just before that. Somehow Jackson had known she was in the room before Ross Taggert had acknowledged her presence. Tall, blond and beautiful, she was every inch a lady and exactly like all the other women he'd ever found attractive and started courting, only to lose them or become disillusioned by them in the end.

What was it with him? he wondered impatiently. Had he inherited some self-destructive gene that drew him toward disappointment that bordered on heartbreak?

He pushed Elizabeth from his mind for probably the ten thousandth time since meeting her. This quest of his to get to know his biological family was enough for him to handle right now. He didn't need attraction and heartbreak to distract him!

The day he'd come, at Ross Taggert's invitation, to discuss the foreman's job, Jackson hadn't been prepared for the similarities between him and his family. Cole had been the first person he'd met, and their shared resemblance had shocked him nearly speechless.

Because Ross had already seen his resume and checked out his references, Ross had hired him within what felt like only minutes. He'd also invited him to dinner at Laurel House, the family's impressive home on the hill beyond the farm's stable compound. Jackson would describe it as a mansion, but Ross called it the house, as if it were a three-bedroom colonial rather than a brick and stone memorial to a proud family's history.

Jackson thought it was a miracle he'd survived that first night at Laurel Glen with his job intact thanks to Elizabeth Boyer's arrival at the dinner party Amelia, Ross's wife, had arranged to welcome him. He'd been nervous going in but he'd been doing fairly well until he'd turned and encountered eyes the color of emeralds staring at him in worried confusion. After that he'd had trouble keeping his mind on the conversation swirling around him.

When they'd been called into dinner, he'd found himself seated next to Ross and across from Ross's daughter, Hope, and her husband, Jeff Carrington, who lived on a neighboring farm. Like Ross and his wife of less than a year, the couple was expecting a baby. The four of them fell into an earlier conversation, but time and again Jackson found his attention snared by Elizabeth, who'd been seated to his left. She wore a light scent that reminded him of the warm sultry evening outside, and it had wrapped itself around him the same way the garden had as he'd approached the rear door to Laurel House that evening.

After a while, he'd noticed Elizabeth wasn't participating in the conversation any more than he was. He'd wondered if she was as distracted and aware of him as he was of her, but he'd tried to dismiss his musings as unimportant. She was clearly Cole's, and he didn't want to poach on his cousin's territory. There was no way he would risk damaging any relationship he might be able to develop with Cole over some society debutante who'd dump both of them in the end anyway.

Then, just when he'd convinced himself he had no choice but to give Ms. Boyer a wide berth, she and Cole left, leaving the rest of the family making comments on their relationship. The family was divided about how serious they were, but they all felt the two were wrong for each other. Jackson told himself he didn't care. Elizabeth was just as wrong for him.

He had a lousy track record with women. Time and again he'd tried to establish long-lasting relationships with what his father disdainfully called city girls.

Why he gravitated toward women fated to disappoint him he had yet to figure out, but he knew it proved he was as slow as they came in the romance department. Even he'd finally learned, however. Women like Elizabeth Boyer were not for him.

Besides, he didn't need anything complicating his already complicated life. He'd come here to find his mother and meet his family. That was all he had the energy to handle.

After that he didn't have enough time to think about anything but accomplishing the next task on his list. By then Cole had diagnosed CJ Larson's mare with West Nile Virus, and a furious round of activity had followed that had lasted for days.

Jackson had had to supervise everything, from scouting possible sites of mosquito infestation to posting men to keep reporters off Laurel Glen property and away from the already skittish livestock.

He'd fallen into bed each night exhausted and sick to death of the smell of mosquito repellent. But at least Elizabeth Boyer hadn't been the only thing he spent his days thinking about.

No. Thoughts of her were merely the *last* ones to go through his head before sleep claimed his nights. Consequently she was the star player in all his dreams, as well.

Evening was approaching when Jackson heard a booming laugh echo down the hill and the thunder of approaching hooves. He looked into the yard to see his cousin, Cole, ride into the compound, trailing an older woman by a length.

"You cheated," Cole shouted, laughter in his voice as he jumped off his horse.

The woman dismounted and smiled mischievously. "That's the prerogative of age, darling boy." She had a voice that was low and a tad rough in a soothing sort of way.

"Shall I have a couple of men take care of your horses?" Jackson asked, approaching them.

The woman turned quickly and stared at him. She didn't say anything for an uncomfortably long time. She just stared. He should be getting used to the shocked reaction everyone had to his resemblance to the Taggerts, but he wasn't. He handled it this time the way he had all the rest, by acting as if he hadn't noticed the similarity or their reaction to it.

The woman blinked, then smiled. "And who would this young man be?" she asked.

"Oh, I'm sorry, Aunt Meg," Cole said.

Jackson's heart, which had begun to quicken with hope, pounded in his chest. This was his mother.

"This is Jack Alton," Cole continued. "He's the guy Dad hired to take Harry Donovan's place. Jack, this is my aunt Meg. World traveler and surrogate mother to all of Laurel Glen."

Jack wondered if his last name would tip her off to who he was, but she just smiled pleasantly at him. He studied her. She didn't look feckless or uncaring—just the opposite, in fact. She had a kind face and a mature beauty he was sure most women would spend a fortune to have. From the smooth way she'd slid off her mount, he could see she still had a dancer's grace. And her wide, open smile told of an outgoing personality that must have aided her stage career.

The career he'd learned she'd abandoned for her niece and nephew. But there was something he might not have considered. How did he know there wasn't another Taggert relative named Meg? After all, he had two aunts called Mary in Colorado, didn't he? He might be getting all excited over the wrong woman.

"Would that make you Meg Taggert, Ross's sister?" he asked.

Her eyebrows climbed, wrinkling her smooth forehead a bit. "Well, yes, it would."

"Ma'am, this may sound like a foolish question but were you in *Hello, Dolly!* on Broadway in the sixties? I think I remember your name from a playbill my parents must have brought home from a trip to New York. It was before my time, of course, but just before I left to come here, I was looking over my mother's effects and I found it in her memory box."

"Actually, yes, I was in *Hello, Dolly!* I was in the chorus." Meg frowned. "Your mother's effects, you say? Then she's deceased?"

Jackson heard the genuine sympathy in her voice, and his opinion of the woman went up another notch. He nodded.

"Oh, I'm so sorry. Where did you say you hail from?"

"Out west, ma'am," he answered vaguely, afraid perhaps his questions had given away too much. "I'd already talked to your brother about the job here, so your name stuck in my head when I saw it in the playbill. It's a small world, they say.''

He hated lying, but he wasn't ready to tell her who he was. Especially not in front of a witness. This was between him and Meg Taggert.

Hoping to change the subject, Jackson quickly asked, "So, Cole, do you want me to have one of the men see to your animals?"

Cole hesitated then sighed. "I'll take care of them. A bet is a bet, and she beat me even if she cheated. I'll see you at dinner, cheater," Cole called after his aunt.

Meg Taggert had an answer for her nephew but Jackson couldn't seem to focus on what they were saying. He was too bowled over by the meeting. Then he heard her laughter floating behind her on the summer breeze as she sailed toward Laurel House.

"Now that your aunt's gone, why don't you let me take care of the horses? You probably shouldn't even have been riding with that separated shoulder of yours,'' he told Cole.

"Oh, it's coming along." Cole glanced after his aunt and rotated the recently separated shoulder a bit, wincing. "But now that you mention it, maybe I did overdo it a little." He turned the reins over to Jackson with a grin. "Besides," he said, a chuckle in his voice, "she really did cheat. Thanks a lot, Jack."

He watched Cole walk toward the barn where he probably planned to check on the recovering mare, then Jackson whistled for a couple of the kids Ross hired from a teen program at the local high school.

He gave orders for the care of each animal then turned and headed for his office. Minutes later he sank into the chair behind his desk, his thoughts on the woman he'd just met.

So that was his mother.

Elizabeth had fled to Laurel Glen and Glory after a particularly nasty scene with her mother. It seemed Louise Boyer had found yet another son of yet another friend who was simply perishing to take her out.

He had money. Gobs of money. And, better yet, he was lonely. He worked eighty hours a week as an associate at O'Connor, Belzer, Creasey and McAllister, one of Philadelphia's top law firms. And he was wife shopping. It was time, he'd decided—the next step if he was going to advance his career.

If only Elizabeth would be charming and smile and be nice, her mother told her. If only she'd bring him up to scratch and marry him, he would surely bail them out of the financial mess her father's poor investments had caused.

At first Elizabeth hadn't been able to believe her ears. Her mother had never before been so forthright about her plans. It told Elizabeth her parents' money troubles were worse than she'd thought. It also sounded annoyingly like the plot of a Victorian novel, Elizabeth had informed her mother. She was not for sale. She'd gone on to explain that she was a woman of the new millennium and her parents' financial problems were not hers.

Two hours later, she was finally feeling human

again. The pasture fence leading into the yard near Stable Two loomed, challenging her and Glory. None of the workers was anywhere nearby, so she gave Glory her head and they flew over the fence—two parts of a whole. She reveled in that moment of weightlessness just before Glory began the downward arc to the ground.

She laughed and patted her seven-year-old Irish draft horse on her gracefully curved gray neck as they slowed to a stop. It had been five long days since she'd had the opportunity to put Glory through her paces, and the wonderful freedom of riding filled her.

"That could be dangerous, Ms. Boyer," Jack Alton declared as he marched up to her. "If you don't care about your own safety at least care about your animal and the handlers. Suppose one of the men had walked in front of you. I don't need another man injured right now, especially because someone got careless."

Irritated, Elizabeth looked at him from her position in the saddle. He was so handsome yet so provoking. And the afternoon had been going so well. Until now! She tilted her head a bit and tried shooting her best imperious look at him. "Mr. Alton," Elizabeth said, mimicking the formal tone he'd used with her. "I was taking jumps like that by the time I was twelve years old. My father is an Olympic equestrian coach. Believe me, Glory was in no danger. I know what I'm doing."

"Fine. But what if someone had walked in your path?"

Elizabeth gritted her teeth. Did he think she was a

complete idiot? "Had anyone been near, I assure you, I wouldn't have made the jump. I have enough brains in my head to check to make sure the yard is empty." She dismounted and glared coolly at him. "If, however, it bothers you this much, I'll only jump this fence when Ross is around. Then you can take your objections up with him, since he is the first one I ever saw do it."

That said, she slapped Glory's reins against his chest. Looking nothing if not astonished, he made what looked like an automatic grab for them as she let go.

"Glory's had quite a workout," she snapped. "After she's been shampooed, kindly see her legs are bandaged. She tends to have a problem with swelling after hard work. CJ Larson knows all about it."

Elizabeth didn't wait to see Jack's reaction to her imperious demands. She pivoted on her heels and stalked toward the clinic to check on CJ's mare, Morning, and to see how Cole's separated shoulder was coming along. Behind her she heard Jack Alton growl, "A real rider takes care of his own mount."

She took a deep calming breath and kept walking. As she approached the big stone barn, she shook her head, and thought about her reaction to Jack Alton. Elizabeth didn't know why she let him get to her, but at least all she'd felt was pure, clean anger. That was a definite improvement.

Through the years she had always been able to either intimidate or ignore the men she couldn't avoid but she found either impossible with this one. She was at least able to console herself with the lack of fear she'd felt. Anger continued to feel good. Really good.

Then a disturbing thought struck. This was the second time anger toward him had overshadowed the uneasiness she felt around Jack. Had she overreacted to his criticism? Been mean rather than righteously annoyed? Was she trying to make him pay some arbitrary price because he'd looked at her with interest and because he made her uneasy—a feeling she hated?

She didn't know, and when she reached the barn it turned out she couldn't divert her thoughts with a visit with Cole. He'd left for his office, having put Georgie Burk in charge of Morning. After a short visit with the sweet-natured mare and older man who'd been at Laurel Glen for years, Elizabeth set out for her car. She'd spent a lot longer than expected riding, which was why she'd jumped the fence. Cutting the few minutes it would have taken to ride around the other stables and barn had seemed worth it, but she hadn't picked up any time after all, thanks to being held up by Jack Alton's lecture. Consequently, she was even later for work at the women's shelter than she would have been if she'd stopped to open the gate!

Nearly everyone assumed she worked at New Life Inn as a volunteer, but it was more for her now—she was getting paid for her work. With her parents' finances collapsing, Elizabeth had finally taken a stand against her father and his demand that she not work for a living. He found it embarrassing. And as always, she found his attitude positively Victorian.

With Meg Taggert for a role model, Elizabeth had broken out of the mold and set out on her own personal road to independence. It was such a good feeling to unlock the door to her office, to go to the bank and cash a paycheck instead of withdrawing from her trust fund, to see a woman she'd help make a fresh start. It was fulfilling.

Hurrying to where she'd parked, Elizabeth turned the corner next to Stable Four and smacked straight into a wall of damp chambray that covered what felt like several square feet of stone hard flesh. Gasping, she stepped quickly back, lost her balance and found herself sitting in the grass.

The way her day had gone so far Elizabeth didn't know why she was surprised when she looked up and found Jack Alton smirking at her, but she was.

"You really need to watch where you're going," he drawled, offering her a hand up.

"And you don't?" she'd demanded. Scrambling to her feet, Elizabeth ignored his hand.

"I'm not the one with the grass stains all over her, ah, seat, am I?"

Elizabeth felt her face heat. The baboon had actually mentioned— "Only because you're a big oaf," she said through carefully gritted teeth and then continued icily. "I wouldn't have thought Ross Taggert would be so careless about the kind of people he hires after what your predecessor put the family through."

Jack's eyes abruptly narrowed and blazed like twin lasers. "Are you comparing me to Donovan? Their old foreman? The one in jail for burning down Stable

Four and for murder? The man who tried to kill Amelia Taggert?''

There might be something about Jack Alton that had her pulse skittering all over the place whenever he was around but, no, she didn't think there was any comparison between him and Harry Donovan. It was just that Jack was so irritating!

''Not necessarily,'' she said, giving him her best frozen glare and backing down only a little, ''but I'd say the verdict is still out on what you're doing at Laurel Glen. You could say I don't believe in coincidence. And neither does Cole, by the way.''

As parting shots went, Elizabeth thought as she slid into her car and cranked the engine to life, that had been right up there with Clark Gable's famed last line of *Gone With The Wind*.

Jackson stood staring after Elizabeth as she tore down the access road toward the entrance arch. That Cole was suspicious wasn't a news flash. But Jackson's ridiculous attraction to Elizabeth would be quite a news flash to the people back home in Colorado. Everyone knew Jackson Alton gave women a wide berth these days and had for the last three years.

Unfortunately, he wasn't as surprised as they would be that he was feeling the way he was. Because he knew what drew him to Elizabeth. She was a beautiful woman and all wrong for him, so it stood to reason he'd be drawn to her—his track record being what it was. There was also no reason not to acknowledge, at least to himself, that he was attracted to her. But there was every reason for him to avoid her like the plague.

She was wealthy, beautiful and involved with his cousin. The fact that theirs was apparently a relationship Jackson could never countenance only proved she was not the kind of woman for him. Besides that, only a fool would repeat a mistake.

He probably wasn't the first guy to be disappointed by a woman, but he had such a long history of romantic blunders. He was forever picking women who wanted different things from life than he did. Women who could never understand the joy he found in hard work or watching a foal come into the world. Women who would never share his faith. The trouble with all his missteps was that each time it happened everyone on the Circle A and in town had known and had felt sorry for him. And that was hard on a man's pride.

Feeling suddenly desolate and alone, Jackson walked to the pasture fence and gazed over Laurel Glen's green fields with their crisscrossing fences. He closed his eyes and sighed. He hadn't spoken to the Lord in weeks. Not since finding out his whole life had been a lie. He hadn't felt God's presence at the little church he'd gone to the Sunday before.

Lord, I'm sorry that we haven't been talking. I feel so alone without You. I guess I've been a little resentful, finding out something like this all of a sudden. I hope You understand what I'm doing here. I just want to find the kind of connection with these people I have with You.

Help me do the right thing. Show me the best way to approach my mother. And Lord, about Elizabeth, could You send a little strength my way before I make an idiot of myself over her?

Chapter Three

Elizabeth pulled into the last parking spot available and looked at the quaint row of stores that formed the center of the little town of Village Green. She loved the historic village with its high wooden sidewalks and eclectic mix of shops. Reaching for calm, she sat for a heavenly moment and let the cool wind blow through her windows. The lovely summer day had been washed clean of humidity and summer's excess heat by a cold front and an accompanying thunderstorm. The light show and dousing had just ended, so the air was as perfect as the quiet moment.

The booming thunder and flashing lightning had been nothing compared to the fireworks she and her mother had created not long before at home. But she'd triumphed, and it felt good. Lance Goodwin Bond would not come to call at her door unannounced the way he had last night with an impression—courtesy of her mother—that he was expected and welcome.

One battle won.

Sighing and giving up on finding any more serenity, Elizabeth climbed out of her low-slung car then leaned in to grab her purse and the sack of letters she'd come to mail. Sometimes she got so tired. Her life had been a series of battles both personal and parental since the day Jason Lexington tore her life to shreds. Why she went on hoping it would change, Elizabeth didn't know. But she had a feeling happiness and contentment were anyone's if they just looked in the right place.

Deep in thought and preoccupied, Elizabeth rooted in her purse for her sunglasses but never found them. From nowhere someone bumped into her, knocking her purse to the ground and sending her back a few steps. She bent automatically to pick up her purse.

"I'll get that for you, Ms. Boyer," a cultured voice said.

"No. That's fine. I can get it," she said, shaking the water off her leather designer handbag. She didn't bother to look up, but assumed it had been the voice of her careless sidewalk mate. As she stood, purse in hand, she realized he'd known her name and found her path still blocked. A man who was perhaps six inches taller than her own five feet seven inches stood staring at her with a look in his eyes that robbed her of her ability to move. Hate and malevolence radiated from him. And she was his target.

"What?" she found herself automatically asking the angry, blond Adonis blocking her path.

"I'm glad you asked. What I want from you is for you to tell me where you've hidden Melissa."

Melissa? The only Melissa she knew was Melissa Hobart. Three months earlier, Elizabeth had been called to the ER by the hospital's social worker to come pick up a domestic abuse victim and offer her shelter. Ugliness hid in all sorts of pretty packages in today's world, Elizabeth thought, staring at Brian Hobart's pretty face and remembering the bruised and broken young woman she'd picked up that day.

Melissa Hobart had a job and was nearly ready to move into her own apartment. Her divorce had been filed last week. She'd moved on. Apparently her abusive husband wasn't ready to let go.

"I don't know what you're talking about, sir," Elizabeth lied. "Please step aside."

"You know exactly what I'm talking about. You run the New Life Inn. That has to be where Melissa is. Look, I just need to talk to her. She won't give me a chance to explain. I just want the chance to patch it up with her. Things are different now. I'm more in control of myself. Her leaving really woke me up."

Brian Hobart smiled then, and Elizabeth understood how Melissa had talked herself into going back to him time and time again after his temper put her in the hospital. But he'd met his match. Elizabeth wasn't fooled by the smile or the speech. She understood about men like Hobart. But she didn't understand how he'd found out where his wife was. Everything about the New Life Inn women's shelter was supposed to be confidential.

"I'm sorry. I can't help you," Elizabeth claimed. "I have no idea what you're talking about, sir. Now if you'll excuse me, I have business in the post office."

Hobart stepped closer and grabbed Elizabeth's wrist in a punishing grip. He did it so smoothly and quickly she doubted anyone realized she had no choice but to allow him to stand so close. And to Elizabeth's mortification she let out a pained and fear-filled whimper. His grip tightened, and her gaze flew to his face.

"Quiet, Ms. Boyer. We wouldn't want to attract a crowd, would we?" This time his smile reminded her of a snake ready to strike. "And, no. I will not excuse you," he said, squeezing so hard Elizabeth thought her wrist would shatter if he tightened his grip anymore. "You tell me where Melissa is and you tell me now."

She stared into his sneering face, her heart leaping into her throat. Repelled, she looked away, frantically hoping to see someone who realized this was not a friendly encounter.

A soothing hand settled gently on her shoulder from behind, and a strong male arm stretched forward and braced against Hobart's chest. "That grip you have on Ms. Boyer's wrist doesn't look real comfortable. Suppose you let go and step back, fella." Jack Alton's suggestion sounded so wonderfully dangerous in his deep voice that Elizabeth's heart leaped with gratitude.

"This is none of your business," Brian Hobart snapped.

"You could take that view, I suppose, but since she's a friend and it doesn't look as if you are, then I'd say we have a difference of opinion. Now, one more time. Step back or I'll put you in the dirt."

Faced with someone his own size whom he couldn't intimidate, Hobart let go and stepped back. He was a typical bully.

"Look, you're a man," he said, his voice a tad anxious. "You should understand how I feel. She's hiding my wife, and I have a God-given right to talk to my own woman. They're brainwashing her in that shelter. She even filed for divorce. She'd never do that without them influencing her."

"Well, now. I don't know if Ms. Boyer is hiding your wife from you or not. And I can't know what's in the young lady's head since I don't know her. But I will agree that I'm a man," Jack said slowly, as if he were addressing a small child. "You, however, I'm not too sure about. Using force on a woman doesn't make you a man. Just the opposite in my book. So I can't really say I could put myself in your shoes. No wife of mine would ever need to hide from me in a shelter." Jack took a step forward. "Now go climb into whatever car you arrived in and get! I'm about out of patience, *boy*."

Brian Hobart walked backward a few steps as if making sure Jack stayed where he was then turned to hurry to his car. He stopped next to his silver Lexus, apparently having found his bravery now that half a parking lot was between him and Jack. He glared at both of them.

"Where do you get off interfering with a marriage? I'll find her and she'll come home with me. You haven't won."

They watched in silence, Jack's hand still on her shoulder, as Brian Hobart got in his car and wheeled out of the parking lot. Only then did Elizabeth feel the tingle of blood rushing into her fingers and the residual ache in her wrist from Hobart's punishing grip. She cradled her hand and wrist, wincing at the pain. To her everlasting embarrassment, she started to shake, and her legs grew weak. She thought she might wind up a heap on the sidewalk, but Jack encircled her with his arms and braced both her elbows.

"That little café looks mighty inviting just about now. Suppose we wander on in there and get ourselves something to drink."

"I—I have to go to the post office."

Jackson glanced at the little clock tower at the edge of the lot. "I'd say you have another couple hours before it closes. Do you really have to go right now?"

Elizabeth shook her head, knowing as well as he did that she'd never be able to stand in line the way she felt at that moment. Besides, for some reason, probably because he'd come to her aid, his presence was comforting. She really didn't want to be without that right now.

"Something cool to drink sounds perfect. I'm sorry

I'm in such a dither. That was such a shock. No one at the hospital is supposed to give out information about the shelter. If its location is compromised…''

Jack led her into the little café, then went to the counter and returned minutes later. She still hadn't managed a clear, concise thought by the time he did. In his hands he had a plastic bag of ice and a towel he'd obviously asked for.

"This should minimize any bruising or swelling," he said then he wrapped the ice in the towel and gently circled her wrist with it, tying the ends of the cloth in a knot. Then he was gone, only to return seconds later with two tall glasses. "Now suppose you tell me about this shelter," he suggested as he sat across from her, putting iced tea in front of each of them. His smile brightened his already bluer than blue eyes.

Elizabeth pushed the thought of his eyes out of her head and forced herself to answer his question. "Maggie O'Neill, the housekeeper my parents had since before I can remember, broke her hip a couple of years ago. While she was in the hospital, she had a roommate. Donna looked as though she had been in a severe car accident. Maggie managed to get her talking a little but it was as if Donna tried to make herself invisible.

"I felt so sorry for her. No one ever came to see her but her husband and he was…intimidating, I guess would describe him best. Donna reverted to being a silent shadow when he was there. He even made Maggie nervous, and she has the heart of a Valkyrie.

Then one day I heard the nurses talking about Donna's injuries. Apparently this wasn't the first time she'd been in the hospital. And each time it had been her husband who'd put her there. She refused to press charges. I asked them why someone didn't help her. They said they had tried to talk her out of going home with him each time but she had nowhere to go.

"Her situation haunted me. I wanted to help her so I went to the room and tried to reach her. I thought I had. We were going to talk more the next day about her coming to stay with me until she was ready to go out on her own.

"I didn't understand many of the things I do now about Donna's situation. An hour with Maggie and me telling her she didn't deserve such treatment and that she could make it on her own just couldn't compete with her husband."

"How so?" Jack asked, looking interested and concerned. It surprised her, but she realized it shouldn't after the way he'd spoken to Brian Hobart. So she went on having a conversation with him she'd never had with anyone else.

"Men like him are very subtle at first," she told him. "They start by undermining the woman's confidence in herself and her ability to make it in life without him. Next they separate their partner from any support structure outside of them. That's why no one came to see Donna. She no longer had friends or family to turn to. She had only him."

"What a shame."

Elizabeth nodded, remembering Donna as if she'd

seen her yesterday. "Very much a shame because by
the time the physical abuse begins the mental abuse
has prepared the victim to accept the treatment as jus-
tified. Even if they don't accept it, they have no one
they feel comfortable turning to. The reason these
men give for their actions is usually that the violence
is the woman's fault. They aren't good enough house-
keepers, mothers—lovers. There's always something
that makes her deserve his wrath. By that time, these
women are so isolated that even if they want to leave
they don't see how they can."

"Did she—"

Hurting all over again, Elizabeth shook her head
and fiddled with the knot Jack had so carefully made
in the towel around her wrist. "She left the hospital
with him that day. Two days later she was in the ER,
but this time he'd gone too far. She died of internal
injuries. If there's a God, Donna's husband will never
get out of prison."

"Oh, there is, and when the State of Pennsylvania
gets done with him, God will be waiting to take
over."

Liking Jack's take on the situation, she nodded and
went on with her story. "I decided I was going to use
my connections and my finance degree to help women
who feel helpless take charge again and build better
lives for themselves. You can't imagine how awful it
is to have someone overpower you and take away
your choices," she said, needing someone to understand why she cared about women like Donna and
Melissa. She couldn't single-handedly prevent the

kind of life-stealing event that had happened to her behind the high school but she could give these women back their lives.

"I take it you succeeded," Jack said, approval in his expression.

Elizabeth nodded. "I raised the money to buy a big old home on one of the most rural roads around here and to fund the kinds of programs women like Melissa need to break free and take control of their lives."

"What is your connection now? Why did Hobart sound so sure that you knew where his wife is?"

"I've kept a low profile about it but I stayed on as the administrator. Meg talked me into it and I'm so grateful she did. It's very rewarding seeing these women become whole, learn real life skills and stand on their own two feet again. They're different people when they leave than they are when they arrive. Because I'm the administrator, I'm also the contact person the hospital social workers call when they need to place a woman in my facility. I took Melissa Hobart from the hospital to the New Life Inn myself."

"New Life Inn. I like that," Jack said, but then he frowned. "Someone must have seen you pick her up and told Hobart."

"I don't see how. I have a routine for pickups. I wait in the hospital's employee lot. It's walled in on all sides, and we do it in the middle of the night when there isn't a shift change. It was nearly two in the morning and no one was around."

A thought occurred to her, and Elizabeth started to

stand but quickly gave up. Her legs were still unsteady.

"Whoa. I don't think you have your sea legs yet. What's wrong?" he asked, a look of concern settling on his handsome features.

"It doesn't matter how he got the information, I have to warn Melissa Hobart."

"Don't you have a cell phone?"

"I left it in my car."

Jack pulled his phone off his belt and handed it to her. She made the call and was relieved that Melissa remained not only steadfast and determined to stay free of her husband, but was angry rather than afraid. Her commute to her job in Center City, Philadelphia, was long, but since her new apartment was just outside the city, it soon wouldn't be. Melissa told Elizabeth she had decided to move in immediately and not wait to buy the rest of her furniture. She had a bed and, to her, camping out in an empty apartment was better than crossing paths with Brian Hobart.

After talking with Melissa, Elizabeth felt calm enough to complete her business in town and leave for the shelter. "Thank you for chasing off the bully," she said as they stood to leave. "I've never been very good with that sort of problem."

Jack chuckled. "I guess I owe you a thank-you, as well."

"Whatever for?"

"Well, for not thinking I'm a bully."

Elizabeth gave him a jaundiced look. "Oh? And how can you be so sure?"

"'Cause, ma'am, you haven't had any problem standing up to me since the day I arrived."

Elizabeth felt her cheeks heat and turned to push open the café door. "Why is it you take such joy in embarrassing others?"

"Not others. Just you. And I was teasing, not trying to embarrass you. Some folks are just plain easy to tease that I can't help myself. And you're one of them. Try not taking yourself so seriously. Life's a whole lot more fun that way. Come on. We'll go to the post office then I'll walk you to your car and make sure Hobart isn't still hanging around somewhere."

Jackson watched Elizabeth drive away a few minutes later. He'd misjudged her in many respects. He'd only asked her about the women's shelter to get her talking so she would be able to focus on something other than Hobart. He'd assumed her involvement was a typical socialite's cursory dabbling in a charity to gain the good opinion of others.

Her deep commitment to the women's shelter she'd appropriately named the New Life Inn surprised him. It was laudable yet troubling, too. It seemed to Jackson that she had a deep personal knowledge of the inner feelings of the woman whose plight had inspired her. *You can't imagine how awful it is to have someone overpower you and take away your choices.*

He couldn't imagine where Elizabeth could have learned such a difficult personal lesson. But the passion in her voice had spoken of just that, and he didn't think a short acquaintance with an abused woman could have affected her as deeply as she'd claimed. Yet she was an unmarried, pampered princess from the highest echelon of society. And since she was involved with his cousin Cole, clearly a man with a kind heart, Jackson didn't think that relationship was the source of her dark knowledge. Whatever the source, he was uncomfortable categorizing Elizabeth as the social butterfly he'd assumed she was.

But Jackson was no longer confident of his judgment where women were concerned at all. He'd judged Elizabeth harshly but hadn't scrutinized others enough. So he had to wonder if his attraction to her was blinding him to obvious faults in the same way it had caused him to overlook her virtues.

The problem was that Elizabeth seemed to be two people. One he understood—the ice princess she showed the world. The other—the warm, caring, socially conscious administrator of a women's shelter—didn't fit with a vain young woman to whom appearance meant everything and who had been handed everything in life.

"Would the real Elizabeth Boyer please stand up?" muttered Jackson as he climbed in his truck and twisted the ignition. With a sigh of disgust, he turned the truck off. He'd come here to pick up a part for one of the tractors, and it had flown out of his head the second he'd seen Hobart grab Elizabeth's wrist.

He was afraid he'd never shake the protective feelings for her that had surged to the fore when he'd sensed her fear from across the lot. And he was afraid that spelled trouble with a capital T.

Chapter Four

Jackson wiped his forehead with a bandanna and looked toward where he knew the sun should be. He shook his head in disgust. Nothing but haze. Again. He hadn't seen the sun in two weeks. Not since the day he'd scared off that weasel named Hobart who'd been threatening Elizabeth. Since then both she and the sun had been making themselves scarce.

Oh, there was plenty of evidence of both but only in a cursory way. The sun stayed behind a thick haze of humidity floating between the great ball of fire and the mere humans currently being boiled beneath its diffused rays. As for Elizabeth, he'd heard Cole was still seeing her, often staying out all night, according to gossip.

And he hated it!

But since he hated gossip, too, and he spent way too much time thinking about the puzzle that was Elizabeth, Jackson firmly put her out of his head once again. Instead of brooding, he climbed on his horse, forcing his mind onto another more safely pondered enigma. Pennsylvania weather.

In Colorado you checked fences in all sorts of weather but it never felt as if you were riding through a blazing steam bath. And back home the only time the sun didn't make an appearance during the day was in foul weather. He chuckled. Then again, this weather was pretty darn foul.

As Jackson turned to trace the fence line along Indian Creek Road, he saw a flash of gold in his peripheral vision. He twisted in the saddle and saw Elizabeth and her horse, Glory, fly gracefully over the fence and ride toward him. He couldn't take his eyes from her flushed face and bright eyes.

"Hi," she said, Glory dancing as she guided the glistening gray horse to a halt. "I'd hoped to see you. I wanted to thank you again for scaring Melissa Hobart's husband off. He hasn't bothered me or her since. I guess having another man tell him to get lost worked."

"Glad I could help." He inclined his head toward her horse. "Glory's been missing you. You haven't been around much these last couple of weeks. I began to wonder if Hobart had become more of a problem."

She shook her head, her blond hair loose and waving slightly as it fell on her shoulders. "I stayed away just in case. The last thing I want is to bring trouble with me to Laurel Glen. The Taggerts have had enough problems these last eighteen months without my adding to them."

"It's hard to believe Harry Donovan would do the things he did because he'd been infatuated with Ross's late wife and wanted revenge on Ross over her death."

"He was after Ross and Cole both. Luckily, he didn't do any permanent damage to the business or the family. He did kill his cohort to keep from being discovered, but at least no innocents were killed. Jeff being paralyzed—in one of Donovan's manufactured accidents—for all those months was bad enough although he says it was the best thing that ever happened to him."

Jackson frowned. "But even though he's okay now, Jeff still lost his chance at the Olympics because of it."

Elizabeth nodded. "Jeff seems to think he learned valuable life lessons he'd never have if his life had kept skating happily onward the way he was. And he says it taught him what he calls an eternal lesson because it made him turn to God. Apparently, to him, that was worth all the pain. He's certainly a different person. I don't know if it's God or Hope, though, since he more or less discovered them both at the same time."

"What was Jeff like before?" Jackson asked, wondering. He'd grown up a Christian, but coming from a small church with a pretty much fixed membership, he'd really never seen someone's life transformed, though he knew it happened all the time.

"Jeff was driven to achieve an Olympic gold medal. He worked hard but he played hard, too, and his friends, except me, Cole and Hope, were mostly from the equestrian circuit. They were all the opposite of Hope, that's for sure, and they disappeared when the going got tough while Jeff was paralyzed. I stayed away, too, but for other reasons.''

''I'd say, given all that, the changes in him must be his relationship with God. His relationship with Hope might never have survived the equestrian world's lifestyle,'' Jackson told her.

Elizabeth stared at nothing, a pensive look on her beautiful face. ''No. No, it wouldn't,'' she agreed, but her thoughts were clearly on something other than Jeff Carrington's conversion.

Had Elizabeth been hurt by Jeff Carrington? Had she been as involved with Jeff as she appeared to be with Cole? If so, it was no small wonder he'd noticed antagonism toward her from Hope.

''So what were your reasons for staying away after he was injured?'' he found himself asking, driven to get to know her in spite of all reason.

''Hope badly misunderstood my relationship with Jeff, and I didn't want to create friction between them. My father was his coach. Jeff and I rarely saw each other away from Pennsylvania unless I flew to an event for a visit. Also my father isn't the most diplomatic man in the world. He said some rather cruel things to Jeff following the accident. Frankly, I was mortified and not sure of my reception in Jeff's home, so Cole kept me up to date on how Jeff was progressing.''

Was her relationship with Cole less than everyone

thought? Was the same kind of misunderstanding happening again? Just then Cole and CJ Larson rode through the hollow below at a fast clip. Their laughter rose, full of joy and camaraderie.

''That's another reason I've stayed away from Laurel Glen these last two weeks,'' Elizabeth said.

She didn't sound angry. In fact, she grinned. Jackson tried to understand that but knew he never would. ''Seeing them doesn't seem to make you angry.''

''Why would I be angry? CJ is a wonderful person. I really like her,'' she said, clearly incredulous.

''Are you this cavalier about the end of all your relationships?''

''Relationship? Cole and I—'' She halted what seemed like mid thought and stared at him. Her green eyes caught fire, then they turned to emerald chips of ice. Jackson regretted his question immediately when he saw how angry she was and when, without another word, she wheeled her mount away and charged the same fence she'd flown over just minutes earlier. As horse and rider once again took flight, he realized what had been out of place from the second he'd seen her coming toward him. She wore no riding helmet. And if he hadn't been so moon-eyed over seeing her again, he'd have noticed and reminded her of safety concerns.

Neither he nor Ross wore helmets, either, but Jackson didn't jump fences, and he rode western saddle. He and the boss had reached an agreement that Jackson, who came from a different tradition of riding, would be exempt from farm rules on this one point.

And Ross owned the place, so he could do as he wanted when he rode. Customers, however, weren't covered by the farm's insurance if they were injured while riding without a helmet. And that father of hers would jump at the chance to sue Ross, if his attitude last month with reporters was any indication.

Jackson decided to follow Elizabeth and restate the rules. If he worried about her safety on the ride back, he assured himself it was only for Laurel Glen's sake. If he once again pondered her odd response to seeing Cole happily absorbed in an outing with CJ, he forced his thoughts elsewhere. And if his mind stubbornly veered to unraveling the enigma that was Elizabeth Boyer, he chalked it up to nothing more than the kind of intellectual curiosity that made man dig up the artifacts of ancient civilizations.

By the time he got to the compound and turned his mount over to one of the handlers, Elizabeth was headed for the parking lot behind Stable Four. Jackson called out but she ignored him, continuing her graceful stalk toward her little car. She was about to slide in when he caught up to her.

Without a thought to the consequences, he reached out and caught her arm. Elizabeth pivoted almost violently and smacked into him. And that was how Jackson found himself with his arms full of desirable, angry woman.

She glared at him, indignation blazing in her gaze, and he did the only thing that for some inconceivable reason made sense to him. He lowered his head and kissed her. Instantly, Jackson regretted his strategy.

Her sharp intake of breath as his arms gathered her close seemed to rob him of air, and the feel of her softness against him just about blew the top off his head.

He'd wondered about her in a lot of ways but hadn't let himself think about this. He'd known this path led to destruction and he'd been right!

But the next moment she stiffened as if she'd turned into an ice sculpture. Then she shoved him away so suddenly and so hard he fell back a couple steps—his mind barely functioning.

"How dare you?" she demanded frostily.

"You didn't seem to mind at first. But I guess the men in your life aren't as interchangeable as I thought. Tell me, did you freeze up like this with Cole after Jeff moved on to greener pastures? How long does it take you to switch to a new man?"

He could see fury catch fire and flash in her eyes. Then as if a switch had been flipped the heat turned icy. And then that infuriatingly cool demeanor of hers took over. "You assume it was Jeff who moved on. Did you know I only went out with him that last time to get an opportunity to connect with Cole? And once I did, Hope was welcome to him. I've never regretted my decision. Good day, Mr. Alton."

Jackson didn't stop her this time. In fact, he stood there staring after her, sorry he'd stopped her in the first place. It hurt. The way she'd frozen in his arms. The way she'd fiercely defended her relationship with Cole. It actually hurt. What had she done to him?

He didn't live in a vacuum. He knew the way of

things in today's world. And because he didn't choose to live that way didn't mean he still didn't want the pleasures other men took for granted. He just didn't choose to reach out and take them. And that didn't mean it was an easy choice. Or wasn't a lonely one.

In the next breath, Jackson found himself spun around and shoved against the nearby pasture fence. Cole's very angry features filled Jackson's vision.

"You leave Elizabeth alone. I won't have her hurt. I've seen you two arguing before but I had no idea what it was about until now. I just saw you grab her and kiss her."

Getting steamed at the direction of Cole's accusation, Jackson shoved back. "What makes you think she didn't want me to kiss her? I don't force myself on women."

"Maybe I've lived a charmed life but I've found most women don't nearly take a guy's head off if they want to be kissed."

Jackson had to give him that. "Okay, point taken, but there was no force. I just kissed her. I guess I thought she wanted it as much as I did. Apparently I was wrong. She pushed me away and I let go. I'm sorry I stepped out of line with your...with Elizabeth," he finished, uncomfortable with defining their relationship with Elizabeth as part of the equation.

Cole stared at him for a long moment. "Look, I've always been protective of her and I probably always will be, but what she does isn't any of my business. I just don't want her hurt. See that you don't." That said, his cousin stalked away.

Jackson was really confused. He leaned against the fence and hooked one heel behind him on the bottom rail, contemplating what had occurred. With the heat of the moment past, he realized that Cole's words hadn't been the warning of a jealous lover but more of an overprotective brother. And Jackson should know what one of those sounded like. He'd been one for twenty-nine years. Why weren't either of them the least bit jealous when they saw the other with someone else? And why would Cole be protective of Elizabeth but not possessive? Was their relationship that open or was it that they had no relationship beyond friendship?

Meg Taggert watched and listened to Act Two of the little drama taking place in the parking area behind Stable Four. When Jack shoved Cole backward, she thought one of them would throw a punch and she'd have to step in, but instead they traded only angry words. When Cole warned Jack not to hurt Elizabeth, he confirmed something she'd begun to believe. Her nephew was using the young woman as a smoke screen to keep other women at bay and his family out of the matchmaking business.

Meg had grown suspicious when Hope told her Cole had openly spoken of kissing CJ Larson right in front of Elizabeth and that Elizabeth hadn't turned a hair. Now she'd witnessed another kiss—this one between Jack Alton and Elizabeth. For some reason Elizabeth's claims about her relationship with Cole rang even less true than Cole's.

Meg got a good look at Elizabeth as she drove past. The young woman wasn't angry—not with those tears so evidently streaming down her face and pain and despair written on her lovely features. There was something quite wrong there, and Meg decided she'd have to think of some way to help.

She also had to decide what to do about Jack Alton of Colorado. A near twin to Cole, he was the age of her lost child, sported Taggert-blue eyes and spoke with the voice of a man so wonderful, and reminded her of a love so deep that all others had paled in comparison ever since.

Meg had waited patiently for three weeks expecting him to come to her with questions. She dreaded them and welcomed them with equal portions of joy and fear. She'd prayed for just such a time when she'd open a door and find the child she'd given to others to raise thirty-two years earlier. Along with the gladness there was dread that he'd be angry and ultimately reject her after she answered his questions.

But thus far Jack had remained in the background doing a fine job as foreman. Tipping his hat in a lovely old-fashioned gesture when he saw her from afar but not approaching her. Meg was known for her patience, but her vast store of it was quickly running out.

She watched as Jack returned to the horse he'd left with one of the handlers. He took the reins and led the gelding to the snubbing post for a wash and a rubdown. He was so very conscientious and straightforward in his dealings with the men and his own duties. She very much admired her son. But she worried about him, as well.

He'd looked confused and troubled standing there against the fence after Cole had left him. But since there was little she could do for him until he came to her, she turned her thoughts toward Elizabeth once again. Perhaps she could help there. Perhaps Elizabeth was ready for an invitation to church.

Meg headed toward the house. She had phone calls to make and a little matchmaking to do. Elizabeth and Jack would make a lovely couple now that she thought about it. She'd foolishly promised Cole to stay out of his and CJ's business, but Jack and Elizabeth…now they were another story altogether.

She wouldn't do much. Maybe just a little push in the right direction for both of them.

Chapter Five

Elizabeth stood at the big window in the living room of the carriage house she'd taken over several years ago, watching the front gate for Meg Taggert's silver BMW to arrive. She wanted to get to the car before her parents saw her leaving at nine o'clock on a Sunday morning with Meg. It was bound to cause questions, and quite frankly Elizabeth wasn't in the mood for a cross-examination. She didn't really feel they had the right to question anything she chose to do with her life. They'd given up that right long ago.

Her mother's sudden interest in her after a lifetime of ignoring her or noticing her only sporadically was grating at best. She was sure the sudden interest was no more healthy than at other times when one or both of her parents had suddenly taken an interest in her. If it had been, Elizabeth would feel different. But theirs was always a self-centered kind of attention she didn't need a psychology degree to know wasn't healthy. Because those times were always about something they wanted from her.

She remembered vaguely her beautiful mother primping her little dresses and showing her off to friends, then turning her over to Maggie in cold anger because she'd gotten her outfit dirty.

Later, when she'd shown a slight talent for riding, her father had become fixated on her winning the gold medal that had escaped him. She'd spent what felt to a child like every waking moment eating, breathing and sleeping event riding. Then in a routine screening at school she'd been diagnosed with slight scoliosis. At eleven and twelve, having to wear a back brace should have been devastating but, other than the discomfort, it had been a relief because she couldn't ride in competitions. Reginald Boyer had lost interest quickly, and the respite had lasted until Jason Lexington's attack brought her to her mother's attention.

And for the next four years, until Elizabeth's coming-out ball, Louise Boyer had schooled her daughter in perfection. Perfect hair. Perfect diction. Perfect posture. Perfect everything!

Then, blessedly, she'd been forgotten by both of them—until now. Now they wanted Elizabeth to magically transform herself into the perfect marriage trap. This time, though, they'd met with an immovable obstacle. Her mother's creation couldn't cast out lures. Her creation couldn't bring a man "up to scratch." Her creation was flawed deep inside where no one could see. Where no one could reach.

Even the creation herself.

Even when she wanted to—in the arms of the only man she'd ever found herself attracted to.

The attraction was so foreign to her she hadn't even realized why Jack made her so much more on edge and nervous than other men did—and those reactions had been bad enough. She'd thought it was instant dislike and had been perfectly happy with her theory. Then Jack rode to her rescue in Village Green and helped her with Brian Hobart. And he hadn't stopped there. He'd taken the time to sit in the café and talk to her until she was calm enough to go off on her own.

She thought Jack was a very nice man, though he seemed to go out of his way to hide it. He certainly hadn't been very nice yesterday. He was a bit of a mystery, but then so, she supposed, was she. Even more so after her performance at Laurel Glen yesterday when Jack had pointed out CJ and Cole riding. In the joy of the moment Elizabeth—glad to be with Jack and glad to see Cole with CJ—had forgotten Cole's lie about the two of them. Then Jack had said something about her attitude that in retrospect sounded remarkably like sour grapes. She'd ridden off because some unreasonable form of logic had short-circuited every brain cell she had, telling her that he should know Cole had lied.

Then, to make matters worse, when he'd caught up to her, he'd kissed her the way he'd clearly been wanting to do and the way she had wanted, too. But like a specter from the bowels of the earth, the heat of his body so near had opened the door to the place where she hid the effects of that long-ago afternoon when a spoiled boy had robbed her of her identity and turned her into a victim. Not wanting Jack to see her fear or the tears of frustration that were fighting their way to the surface, she'd confirmed all his suspicions and much more just to get away from his penetrating gaze.

Elizabeth shook off her dark thoughts as Meg's BMW careened through the gate, disappeared for a few seconds, then screeched to a halt below the window. She tooted her horn, and Elizabeth waved then picked up her purse, trying to settle her a nervous stomach. At that moment she didn't know what had possessed her to agree to go with Meg. The only times in her life she'd been to church had been for weddings and funerals.

Of course, yesterday Elizabeth had been home and crying for about an hour when she'd answered the phone to Meg's reassuring voice. That could be one reason. She had to admit any suggestion that might provide a direction for her search for peace would have been welcome at that point. She knew there had to be something out there to bring her a little respite and to wipe away the feeling of Jason Lexington's hands on her. Whether Elizabeth would find her answers at church remained to been seen.

By the time they rolled into the parking lot of the Tabernacle, Meg's church, Elizabeth found herself relaxing in the face of the older woman's friendly chatter. The pastor was Jim Dillon, a nice-looking man in his late thirties or early forties. She'd met him first at

Jeff and Hope's wedding last August and again in November when Ross and Amelia were married. Still no one was more surprised than she when he recognized her.

"Elizabeth. Right?" he asked as he took her hand. "Cole's friend?"

"Yes. How could you remember? We only met twice before."

Jim Dillon shrugged and jostled the slightly fussy infant cradled in his arm. The little vision in pink looked up and gave her father a toothless grin. "Probably because we met at weddings. Other than baby dedications I like weddings the most of all my extra duties as a pastor." The identical infant in his wife's arms flailed her hand into Elizabeth. "This is my wife, Holly. And the budding gymnast she's holding is Rachel. This is Leigh. I think she's going to be the bookish type."

The young boy standing next to Jim Dillon snorted and spoke in a surprising British-sounding accent. "Dad, she can't even hold a book yet without ripping it to pieces."

They all laughed when Jim shrugged sheepishly. "Well, she's fascinated with the tearing sound. You have to give me that. Elizabeth, we're glad to see you here, and I hope you're blessed by the service," he said and greeted a large family coming up the walk as if they were old friends.

The rock music and singing as they entered wasn't what she thought of as hymns, but the sound and words were very moving. She could see these people felt their faith keenly, and that in itself made her more than curious. Minutes later, when Jim Dillon approached the stage, smiling and with a spring in his step, she knew he was exactly where he belonged in the universe. If only she could figure out the same thing for herself.

Deep in thought, Elizabeth missed a great deal of what he said after a few lighthearted lines that had laughter rippling through the congregation. Toward the end of his sermon Jim Dillon said something funny about Saint Peter's predilection toward putting his foot in his mouth, and a low chuckle from off to her right drew her attention.

If lightning had suddenly sparked through the room, Elizabeth couldn't have been more surprised. Jack Alton was in church. And the Tabernacle of all churches. She'd heard Cole's opinion of the congregation, and while it had been meant sarcastically, it had also been something of a compliment to its members. This was not a church for the faint of heart or someone into relativism. This was a back-to-basics kind of church, holding to traditional moral values and strict adherence to biblical principles. But then again he had not discounted the idea that God had changed Jeff Carrington. He'd supported it.

So what did all that say about Jack Alton?

Later, standing with Meg enjoying a cup of tea in a quiet corner of the church hall, Elizabeth voiced that question to Meg.

"I think it says he's a good man," Meg replied. "At least that's what I'm counting on."

Elizabeth frowned at the cryptic answer. "Counting on it?" she asked, then before Meg could clarify what she'd meant, Elizabeth understood what Meg must be referring to. "Oh, yes. Of course. He'd be trustworthy, and in his position at Laurel Glen that would be important."

"Something like that," Meg answered. "So what do you think of him?"

Elizabeth tried to sound unaffected and disinterested. "He and I got off to a bad start. We had several altercations. But then he helped me when a man accosted me in Village Green about the shelter. Jack sent him on his way and he talked me into sitting with him in the café because I was badly shaken. We had a nice chat. But..." Hesitating, Elizabeth squeezed the bridge of her nose, not accustomed to confiding in anyone.

"But?" Meg prodded.

Needing advice and to confide in someone, Elizabeth pressed on. "Yesterday, when I was at Laurel Glen, Jack said some things about Cole and me. Meg, I don't know if Cole has set the record straight with your family the way he promised to, but I need you to understand about us. He and I are only friends. And friends is all we've ever been. It was the same with Jeff. I know Hope misunderstood about Jeff and why I was with him at that dance she'd asked him to. I was there to see Cole, and that was only to repay an old debt to him."

Meg raised her left eyebrow. It was such a Taggert trait that it made Elizabeth smile. "It was you he was with that night in the police car, wasn't it?'' Meg asked.

Elizabeth nodded, feeling her cheeks heat. ''He picked me up after he stole it, then he made me see I was being foolish about some things.''

''I'd just about figured that out and more,'' Meg said, setting down her cup and plate on a nearby table. ''It's our fault Cole confirmed the families' suspicion about your relationship. I fear he did it to keep us from matchmaking. Had we not assumed… But, in our defense, my nephew and Jeff had or still have certain reputations where women are concerned, and your parents travel in what could be called the fast lane, so we just assumed you—'' Meg halted again and shook her head. ''It was wrong to judge you on appearances. I'm so sorry. And I'll certainly spread the word within the family and to a certain foreman, too, if that would help.''

Thinking about the way she froze in Jack's arms, Elizabeth wasn't sure she wanted him aware of how available she was. A profound disappointment fell over her. If only she'd found the magic elixir inside the Tabernacle. She'd found a measure of peace during the hour and a half of the service, but now the old familiar brittle tension had begun creeping back.

''You seemed to enjoy the service,'' Elizabeth heard Meg say. ''Would you like to come with me next week?''

Elizabeth smiled. An hour and a half's worth of peace and tranquillity was better than nothing, wasn't it? ''I'd like that. Yes,'' she said.

"And how are you two lovely ladies today?" Jack Alton asked from behind her. Elizabeth gasped and dropped her cup. The contents splashed, and Meg jumped to avoid being sprayed.

"I'm so sorry, Meg," Elizabeth said. She grabbed a stack of napkins and stooped to mop up the spill.

Jack was on the floor across from her in a split second, taking the napkins from her, mopping up the spill. "No, here. Let me get this. It was my fault for startling you. I'm sorry." He looked into her eyes, and in his a quiet kind of sadness brewed. "'I'm sorry' is all I ever seem to say to you."

"Well, I can see I'm suddenly superfluous around here," Meg said from somewhere above them. "I think I'll mingle, dears, and leave you two to your apologies and the cleanup. Elizabeth, I'll meet you at the front of the church…whenever. Ta!"

The spill sopped up, Jack stood and bent to take her hand. Elizabeth reached out, surprising herself with her desire to touch his solid strength. Once she was on her feet, he released her hand and looked around for a trash can, which was across the room near the food. Elizabeth was surprised to feel bereft of his touch.

When he returned to her side with a fresh cup of tea for her, she accepted it with a smile and asked him, "What brings you here?"

Elizabeth was curious and maybe just a little hopeful to hear his reply. She didn't know much about being a churchgoer but she was sure it said something about a man when he came to church on his own with no woman prodding him.

"Here as in the Tabernacle? I guess the companionship of fellow believers, mostly. And the lessons I learn about life from the sermons."

Disappointment made her frown. That wasn't what she'd come there looking for. Was she once again on the wrong path? "Nothing else? You don't find anything deeper here?"

"Deeper?" he asked, his expression thoughtful at first then a bit guarded.

"Now it's me who's sorry. That was too personal a question."

He shook his head. "No. No, it's fine. You're right. I just didn't think you'd be interested. Things in my life are a little up in the air right now. I made some decisions, but I didn't ask the Lord about them first. Every time I've ever done that it's backfired on me. So I guess I'm looking for a little peace, a sense that right now I'm where I belong. What brings you here?"

"Meg invited me and..." she hesitated and shrugged. There was only so much she could say without letting him know what an emotional mess she was. "I'm not altogether sure."

She could tell he was as unsatisfied with her answer as she had been with his first one. Before he could ask another question she wanted to clear up the mistaken impression he had of her. She should have done it yesterday and not lied to cover her fear and vulnerability.

''I lied to you, Jack,'' she said in a rush before she could chicken out. ''Cole and I are friends. That's all we've ever been. He's terribly attracted to CJ but afraid of hurting her and, I think, of being hurt himself. He set me up as a barrier between them. That's one of the reasons I've been making myself so scarce.''

Which, she thought now that confession time was over, she should do once again. There was no way she could tell him about Jason Lexington or the fear he left her with. There was no way she could stand there and watch his eyes dim with distaste the way her father's had when her mother told him what had happened to her in the woods near the school. She couldn't stand there feeling dirty when she wanted to be pure and untouched by ugliness.

''I have to go. I don't want to hold Meg up. Maybe I'll see you at Laurel Glen. Thanks for the new cup of tea.'' She turned and fled the room.

Chapter Six

Jackson watched in frustration as Elizabeth fled his presence for the second time in two days. What was it with her, he wondered as he sank to a nearby bench. Or was it him?

He honestly didn't know.

The only thing he did know was that he was more confused than ever. Simple logic said Elizabeth wouldn't have bothered to lie in the first place unless he'd made her angry or hurt her. The thought that he had hurt her made him feel pretty lousy, but at least his opinion of her mattered. And she wouldn't have bothered to admit the lie unless she wanted to set the record straight, adding to his conviction that she was as interested in him as he was in her.

But then why had she frozen when he'd kissed and held her?

Could she be attracted to him but feel he was beneath her? It wouldn't be the first time. Was she fighting her feelings because she saw him as little more than a glorified farmhand? She had once reminded him that Cole was part of Laurel Glen and Jackson was there because he was being paid for his time.

But if she thought he wasn't good enough for her, why clear up the misunderstanding about Cole and her at all?

"Now there is the face of one confused young man," his mother said.

Jackson looked up, wondering for a split second when he'd begun to automatically think of her as his mother. Then he looked into her blue eyes—that familiar blue—and saw amusement and caring.

"Just a guess, but most of the time that sort of look goes hand and hand with *holding* hands. With a woman. Am I right?"

Jackson nodded. "Elizabeth. But I'd heard she and Cole were deeply involved."

She waved a careless hand. "Patently untrue. All of it gossip. I've heard the men say things. I've seen the elbowing and proclaiming of Cole as the luckiest man in Chester County."

"She said as much today, but yesterday…yesterday I assumed she was and—"

"Ah, dear boy. It is foolish beyond imagining to ever assume anything where women are concerned. You aren't capable of thinking like a woman. It's the testosterone. It poisons your minds before you're born so none of you are capable of thinking like us."

Jackson couldn't keep the grin off his face. "I'd wondered. Thanks for sharing that."

"There are a few other things I think we need to share. Mind if I sit?"

Jackson jumped to his feet. He wanted to sink through the floor. He couldn't believe he'd sat there like a lump. His grandmother would have handed him his head if she'd seen him act in such an unmannerly fashion. He raked his hand through his hair. "I'm sorry. Please. Sit. I'd love any advice you can give me. I'm…confused."

"I could see that from across the room and I can't resist trying to help. I tried. Really, I did, but my self-control isn't what it once was. Let's start with Elizabeth then move on to other things."

He frowned. "Other things?"

"I'll get to that soon enough. First Elizabeth. I don't imagine you're aware that when she drove off yesterday she was in tears. Over an hour later, in fact, when I called to invite her here today, I could tell she was still crying."

Jackson's heart fell. "I didn't mean— No, that isn't it. I didn't think anything would reduce Elizabeth Boyer to tears."

"Exactly. You didn't think. You assumed. A lot of us have. And we've all been wrong. I began to get to know Elizabeth about a year ago. I've found that beneath a…a facade, if you will, she is not only a sensitive young woman but I fear she is rather emotionally fragile. I haven't found out why, exactly, but I think Cole knows. He is as protective of her as he was of Hope, and maybe even a little more so. I know he had words with you yesterday after Elizabeth tore down the drive.''

Jackson thought about that encounter once again and was more sure than ever that Cole had been playing a big-brother role. "He warned me not to hurt her. Not to stay away. Just that he wouldn't stand by and see her hurt or upset. I didn't intend to hurt her. Cole doesn't trust me, though, so I'm not sure he believed me.''

Meg crossed her arms and fixed him with a steely blue stare. "Now why do you suppose he would feel that way?''

He was tempted to shrug, but it felt too much like lying. He wasn't sure if he was ready to admit who he was or why he was at Laurel Glen, especially in such a public place. "I imagine the way I look.'' He hedged.

"Ah, yes. Your looks.'' Her lips formed a wistful little smile. "And your voice, by the way.'' Her voice broke, and she cleared her throat before continuing. "But you couldn't know about that. So tell me, Jack, why have you come to Laurel Glen? Did you come looking for answers, or revenge, or do you want me to believe that it was pure coincidence?''

Jackson could feel his pulse begin to pound. Why had he thought she wouldn't put two and two together? "No, it's not an accident. I came looking for answers, not to cause you any problems. And I wanted to meet my mother. My family.''

Meg arched one eyebrow. "I thought I'd given you both. A good Christian family. And a mother.''

"You did. But the whole package only lasted four years. Mama died of cancer a year after giving birth to my sister, Crystal." The old anger with his father built but he fought it down not wanting to upset Meg. "My father couldn't—can't—get past his grief. In a lot of ways, it's been like he opted out on most of life except making a success of the Circle A. I guess because it was her family's ranch. Her mother still lived there when Mama died. She raised us. She was a feisty old gal. Half Native American, of the Cheyenne tribe. She married Mama's father when intermarriage was a lot more taboo than it is today, but I never saw her accept less than equal treatment."

"Have you always known about your adoption?"

Jackson shook his head, remembering and relating that life-altering afternoon in the studio. "I never questioned the way I look. I suppose I should have. I didn't resemble anyone in the family, but Dad does have blue eyes. Being adopted never occurred to me. I guess because Crystal looks so much like Grandmother and Mama."

"They were supposed to name you Wade Jackson after your father."

"They did, mostly. My full name is Jackson Wade Alton. College friends shortened it to Jack. So that's what I gave Ross as my name. I wasn't trying to be dishonest. I didn't know how much your family knew and I didn't want to cause you any embarrassment."

"I understand and I thank you." She looked around. They were still very much alone in the back corner of the hall. ''I suppose here's as good a place as any. You said you have questions.''

Jackson nodded. ''One of the things I found that afternoon was the ring. I suspect it was your engagement ring. I managed to answer some of my questions about you and Wade Jackson, my father, on my own. I know he died in the Vietnam War and that he was a pilot. I assume you loved him very much. What I don't understand is why you gave me up and why you left your ring with me.''

He saw a great deal of pain flash into Meg's expression and then it was in her voice. ''Oh, I loved him. He was the embodiment of the word *hero*. And I gave you up for the same reason. I met him in New York when I was barely eighteen. I'd gotten lucky with a break as part of the cast of *Hello, Dolly!* Wade was essentially alone in the world, having lost both his parents a few years earlier. He was between tours of duty. I was also alone. I'd burned my bridges with my father over the career I chose.

''I found out I was pregnant after he'd left for Saigon. My letter didn't reach him before he was shot down. I had only a distant cousin to turn to. I went to her when I lost my spot because I couldn't dance anymore. It was in Colorado that I found the Lord. I loved you already for being part of Wade and our love. It was a different world then, Jackson. I loved you too much to raise you with a stigma of illegitimacy and without a real family. It hurts more than I can say that you didn't have that.''

''No. No, don't feel that way. I did have a good

life. Dad was the best father he could be. It's funny, but leaving the Circle A and coming to Laurel Glen gave me a lot of perspective. Yes, emotionally he's been absent. But he was always there—a male presence in my life. Most important, though, he gave me the Lord. I only had Mama for four years but I remember her. Her smile. The way she smelled and the sound of her singing and her laughter. And I had Grandmother.''

He smiled, knowing the smile was tinged with sadness. ''It wasn't perfect but then life rarely is. Look at Ross and Cole, for instance. They fight like cats and dogs most of the time. Yet who could want a better father than Ross?'' He shrugged. ''Apparently Cole, and I'm sure he has his reasons. Just like I'm sure Ross has his for jumping down Cole's throat practically every time Cole opens his mouth.''

''Thank you,'' Meg said, blinking back tears. ''You'll never know what a double loss it was for me when my father died not two years after I gave you up. To know all these years that Ross would have welcomed me back and I could have had you in my life.''

She shook her head. ''But I don't know how we would have survived for even that short amount of time. I've told myself thousands of times you were better off with the life I thought I gave you.''

''You did give it to me.''

Her expressive brows drew together. ''Then why did you come looking for me?''

''Because I needed to know you. I'd had Mama.

I'd had Grandmother. But there's an empty place in my heart for a mom," he replied, and shot her a nervous grin. He felt as if he was proposing. In a way, he guessed he was. He was after all asking someone to take a permanent place in his life. "Interested in applying for the job?"

She sniffled, and tears filled her eyes, but the smile on her face spoke of nothing but joy. "Oh, yes." Her voice trembled just a little. "Nothing would make me happier. I've dreamed of this day for thirty-two years."

Jackson realized he was seeing her through a sheen of his own tears and quickly scrubbed them away with the heel of his hand. "Great. That means a lot. If you want to keep this just between us, I'll understand. I don't want to hurt your reputation or standing in the community or with your family."

Meg squeezed his hand. "Thank you for worrying about me. I don't think that will happen, but I'd like a little time to decide how to tell everyone."

"Then this is our secret until you say otherwise."

She inclined her head and studied him for a long moment. "Would you mind a little more motherly advice about Elizabeth?"

He grinned. This really was great! "Shoot," he told her.

"Okay then. I think you need to know that Elizabeth hasn't had a storybook life, either. She was something of an ugly duckling born to a couple of spoiled swans. She was largely ignored by her mother until she suddenly blossomed at thirteen or fourteen and Louise took her on like a project. Her mother was nothing more than a sporadic etiquette, elocution and grooming teacher over the years and, from what I understand, Reginald only noticed her as a young child when he thought he could shape her into an Olympic-caliber event rider. She had the poor taste to develop back problems that made his dream an impossibility. Perhaps you should keep that in mind when dealing with her. Sometimes I'm not sure what Elizabeth sees when she looks in a mirror, but I don't think it's the beautiful young woman she is.''

Elizabeth stared into mirror over her dressing table. If she didn't get some sleep soon, there would be no way she could appear in public. The dark circles under her eyes defied cover-up. She looked like she'd gone ten rounds in a boxing ring—and lost.

Night after night she lay in bed replaying Jack's kiss and those few seconds of joy before the panic took over. She rethought and revamped each moment she'd spent with him, wishing she could go back and relive them all—change them all. Wishing she could go back even further and laugh off the taunts of cruel classmates, be suspicious of Jason Lexington, go to biology lab rather than be flattered by his attention.

Shaking her head, Elizabeth picked up the concealing stick, knowing Cole was on his way. He'd sounded upset, and there was no way she could turn him away. But she also knew him. If he noticed anything wrong, his concerns would take a back seat to hers.

Her last conversation with him had been yesterday afternoon, and encouraging. She'd called to see if he'd asked CJ Larson out on a date, but casually so as not to get her hopes up.

"I did it," he'd said.

Elizabeth had laughed at how nervous he sounded. Who would believe ladies' man Cole Taggert was anxious over an upcoming date? "I take it I'm no longer your safety net," she said.

"I wouldn't go that far. I don't want her to get hurt if it turns out that I don't feel all for her that I should. I thought I'd just sort of avoid the subject of you until I was more sure of where I'm headed."

She hated to increase those nerves of his but she would have felt worse had she not told him what she was thinking. "I just thought I should warn you. I've sort of been rethinking our conversation. I'm not sure someone like CJ can spend time with a man she's attracted to and not at least hope they have future. Go slow. You know?"

"I'm not about to rush her into bed," he snapped. "I'm not that out of touch with who she is."

"A kiss for someone like CJ could be as intimate as a whole lot more for the rest of us." Elizabeth heard the sadness in her voice.

"Since when do we put you in a category different from the one Hope and CJ belong in? Just because you have an unearned reputation doesn't make it a real one."

It was an old debate, and they'd never agree. It wasn't about what anyone said or thought, it was about what she felt. "We aren't talking about me. We're trying to safeguard CJ's heart until you're able to risk your own. So have a good time. Have lots of laughs. Just don't get too serious too fast."

Elizabeth finished with her makeup brush and huffed out a deep breath. What had gone wrong on his simple dinner date?

Fifteen minutes later Cole sat glowering at her. "Okay, let me get this straight," he said. "You want me to ask CJ to attend the charity dance the night before the Graystone Cross-country." He shook his head. "Elizabeth, I just got through telling you I've decided not to pursue CJ further till I'm more sure of me."

"And I told you you're an idiot!" She shot the words back.

Cole crossed his arms stubbornly. "As for that race or whatever Graystone and your father want to call it, you know how I feel about that event—"

Elizabeth tuned him out. She was so tired of having to defend her father. "Well, not everyone at Laurel Glen seems to agree with you. Your father entered this year with Ross's Prize."

Cole went pale. "That isn't funny, Lizzie," he snapped.

Elizabeth bristled. It was true that a pain inflicted by a loved one hurt more than one from a stranger. Frizzy Lizzie, they used to taunt before her mother's miracle workers conditioned her flyaway hair. She could see the instant apology in Cole's eyes but she wasn't in the mood to hear it. She smacked the fashion magazines she'd been looking through onto the coffee table. About to storm away, she found herself held in place when Cole grabbed her hand.

"I'm sorry."

"That was uncalled for, Cole."

"I know and I'm really sorry. I guess I forgot you're not supposed to shoot the messenger. Look, I've got to go talk my father out of this."

She saw his panic and knew he was really afraid for his father. Maybe it *was* too dangerous. She'd never gotten involved in anything to do with the Graystone. But Cole was on a fool's mission. Why didn't he see it? "When was the last time you talked your father out of anything? Why waste your time? Better to spend your time remembering that Jeff and Hope will be going to that charity dance because Graystone's daughter is one of their students. And obviously Amelia and Ross will be going since he's a participant. That's going to leave CJ sitting at home, as usual, while all her friends are off dancing the night away. Either that or Jack Alton will take her. I understand Ross bought enough tickets for his professionals and his whole family."

Cole gritted his teeth, clearly trying to hide how much the idea of Jack and CJ upset him. He stood. "If you'll excuse me, I'm going home to tell my father that this is one family member who isn't going to fall in line with his plans and condone Graystone's suicide race."

She adopted her bored-socialite act. He was clearly

not going to take her advice, and she wasn't going to let him see how upset the idea of Jack seeing CJ made *her*. She sat down and picked up her magazines again. "Fine," she said. "Just remember it's your fault if CJ goes with Jack."

Chapter Seven

Jackson called to Cole when he saw him stomping across the compound toward the barn. He looked like a man on a mission, but Jackson was on a mission, as well. There was a big shindig, and he wanted to take Elizabeth. It was insane, completely insane. But after their talk at church last week she was all he could think about. Oh, who was he trying to kid? She'd been on his mind since the day he'd met her.

His problem was even though Elizabeth said she and Cole were only friends, Jackson worried that she'd go with Cole out of habit. So he had to get Cole out of the way.

He'd foolishly promised his mother he'd try to find some way to give Cole a shove toward CJ Larson. Meg had decided the two were perfect for each other. Jackson had no idea if she was right, but if he could convince Cole to ask CJ, it would be perfect as far as he was concerned. Because if Cole asked CJ, then Cole couldn't ask Elizabeth.

"Is there a problem?" Cole asked when Jackson caught up to him.

"Problem? No. I just don't want to step on your toes. Your father told me I'm expected to attend some sort of affair next Saturday night. He hinted that he'd like me to bring a guest and, well, if you're not going to be asking CJ, then I thought I would."

Cole's face took on the look of a thundercloud about to burst forth with lightning aimed straight at Jackson. "Actually I *do* intend to ask her," he growled.

Gotcha! Jackson could hardly fight the urge to grin. "Okay," he drawled. "Well, then I guess I'll give Elizabeth Boyer a call. Man, oh, man, you surely do seem to have a monopoly on all the prettiest women around these parts. I just wondered which one you'd asked out for that night. Thanks for the heads up," he said.

Still trying to keep a smirk from tipping his lips, Jackson saluted Cole with his Stetson and walked away. He could feel his cousin firing lightning bolts at his back. Cole's anger made Jackson want to laugh out loud. He couldn't wait to tell Meg and maybe even Elizabeth what he'd done. He'd just leave out his own motivation.

Who knew? It might just soften Elizabeth up enough that she'd agree to go to the dance with him. A guy had to make points where he could, didn't he?

Especially when that guy had screwed up as much with a woman as he already had!

Elizabeth had stayed away from Laurel Glen this whole week. He had no idea if she was avoiding him or if she was trying to strengthen Cole's relationship with CJ.

Which left him wondering when he'd get a chance to talk to her before the charity ball. A phone call seemed inappropriate after the way they'd parted. He didn't feel right showing up at her home to ask her to attend. And he had no idea where the New Life Inn was located, so he couldn't stop by and visit her at work.

After the Sunday morning church service the next day in the Tabernacle's church hall, the perfect opportunity presented itself. He'd seen Elizabeth come into the sanctuary with his mother again this week. It gave him hope for Elizabeth's quest for answers in her life. She was seeking God. Her questions last Sunday had pointed him to that conclusion, and her return this week confirmed it. He prayed she'd find what she was after and that she'd agree to attend the charity dance with him. While he was at it, he also prayed he wasn't making a huge mistake by pursuing her.

When the service ended, he followed the two women into the church hall. He didn't hang back but approached them right away. Elizabeth looked up as he crossed the room. Her green eyes lit with what looked at first like happiness, but then she quickly looked away. Jackson didn't let that stop him.

"How are you two lovely ladies this morning?"

"Wonderful. Thank you, Jack. And wasn't Pastor Dillon wonderful today?" Meg said. "Whenever he uses his own rocky past as an example, he always gets right to the heart of the matter. I swear there wasn't a dry eye in the house when he was talking about the night his teenage sister overdosed and died. Such a tragic life he led as a youngster."

Jackson knew he might have had a life parallel to the nightmare one Jim Dillon had lived were it not for his young mother's selflessness in giving him to people more emotionally and financially equipped to raise a child. He could tell she still felt guilty because the mother she'd selected for him had not lived long. He imagined she also felt a terrible sense of loss because she had sacrificed being his mother for what she now saw as an empty gesture. The rift between him and his father caused by Jackson's search for her had upset her, as well. She tried to hide it, but he was unusually attuned to her feelings.

"His sermon reminded me how lucky I was to grow up with all of the love and support I had, not to mention a beautiful ranch to roam," he said carefully, willing her to believe him. "Frosted as I am at Dad, I think I'll call and talk to him later today."

Meg put her hand on his forearm. "I'm so glad. Could you do me a favor and keep Elizabeth entertained for a few moments? I need to talk with Pastor Jim about something."

"It'd be a pleasure as long as Elizabeth doesn't mind my company."

"I—I— No, of course, I don't mind," Elizabeth replied.

"Later, dears," Meg said and floated away toward Jim Dillon.

"Isn't she wonderful?" Elizabeth's voice held a wistful note that was tinged with pain. "Sometimes I find myself wishing she were *my* mother."

Jackson suddenly realized how lucky his life had been. He might have grown up without a mother for twenty-eight of his thirty-two years but he'd had three wonderful women in his life. Meg might be the newest but she'd been the first, as well. Martha Alton's loving presence was still in his heart along with Grandmother's take-no-guff affection. All in all he'd had a rather well-rounded life. And as for his father, he may not have been the best but he'd offered guidance and discipline and had certainly added more to Jackson's upbringing than Wade Jackson had been able to.

Putting thoughts of his life aside, Jackson watched the longing on Elizabeth's face as her eyes tracked Meg across the room. Meg's description of Elizabeth's parents had seemed a bit harsh but seeing the yearning in her expression, Jackson thought she might have been excessively kind.

"I take it you don't get along with your mother?" he asked.

"I'm a great disappointment to my mother. Always have been. I grew tired of trying to please her years ago and decided to accept my mediocrity. Lately she's grown impatient with me. Now she considers me a failure." Elizabeth shrugged. "I'm trying to decide if it's true or if perhaps it's she who failed me."

"From where I sit, you are no failure."

She smiled, and Jackson could have sworn the sun brightened.

"Why, thank you, Jack. I do believe that's the first compliment you've ever paid me."

"Well, it shouldn't have been. I've been thinking complimentary thoughts on and off since we met." He grimaced. "Unfortunately, I only voiced the ones influenced by misunderstanding and gossip. I'm sorry. I'd like the opportunity to make it up to you and to get to know you better."

Expression grave, she stared at him. "I'm not sure—"

Before she could voice her doubts, Jackson rushed on. "There's a charity shindig at some manor next Saturday, and the boss wants all the senior staff to attend. He paid a bundle for two tickets for me, and I'd like to take you. Cole asked CJ," he added, in case she thought Cole might ask her.

Elizabeth blinked, and a frown creased her forehead. "Now that's a surprise," she said. "Yesterday he told me he wouldn't be going at all. He was adamant. Since Cole's one of the most stubborn people I've ever met, I can't imagine what changed his mind. I tried to get him to ask her but he wouldn't budge."

Jackson grinned. Points. "Well, I sort of cornered him into it," he told her, and went on to explain the way he'd conned his cousin.

Elizabeth chuckled, but then her expression became

grave, as if she'd remembered a concern. "It's wonderful that he wanted to take her but I'm afraid it might backfire—that's why I backed off and didn't mention it again. CJ's a very brave woman, but bravery isn't going to help if she dresses all wrong for the occasion."

"Do you think Cole cares?"

Elizabeth's eyebrows arched, and her eyes widened. "Cole? No. I'm worried about a couple of piranha who have been waiting for Cole to misstep. My father mentioned that they've decided to attend this year, though they never have before. I'm afraid their acceptance is tantamount to a declaration of war because Cole hasn't cooperated by making a mistake on his own. You can bet they'll circle around his date. I don't think the criticism would hurt CJ but it might make Cole angry on her behalf. He tends to act first and think of consequences later."

Jackson frowned. "I think you may be wrong about CJ. She seems to think Cole prefers—" He hesitated, trying to decide how to say this.

"Me? Or my type?"

"Both."

"She's wrong. Cole's scared to death of CJ because she matters to him. The last woman he cared that much about died in front of him when he was fifteen. Believe me, it isn't easy to get over traumas from the teen years. They last a lot longer than most people believe."

Why did that sound as if she were no longer talking about his cousin? His cousin! He wished he hadn't brought Cole up at all. Now Elizabeth looked sad and, though she denied it, there was some kind of a bond between Cole and Elizabeth. He was always between them, and now Jackson had to ask her to the charity dance a second time. "So, ah. About the invitation—"

"I'd love to go," she said in a rush as if she'd had to force out the words.

Jackson blinked. "Great. Well, great. I guess you should tell me where you live. I'd better not ask Cole. He didn't look too thrilled with me last time he saw me."

Why did I mention Cole again?

Elizabeth smiled—a little nervously, Jackson thought—and gave him directions. All week Jackson thought about the anxiety that had creased her smooth forehead. He didn't know if it was a good sign or not but he didn't like the idea of a night in his company causing Elizabeth even one second's distress.

Saturday morning rolled around, and Elizabeth woke with a feeling of impending doom. She couldn't shake her worry over Cole's plan to attend the Graystone Ball with CJ. She knew if left to her own devices CJ Larson would wind up fish food for Mitzy and Alexandra Lexington. And if that happened Cole would more than likely commit an unpardonable social sin on CJ's behalf. There seemed nothing to be done short of Elizabeth going to Laurel Glen and telling CJ what to wear.

That was how she found herself knocking on the

pretty, diminutive trainer's door later that morning. She was there on more than a mission of mercy, she told herself, feeling out of her element. She owed Cole, and in a way she had created the problem years earlier by letting herself be flattered by Jason Lexington's attention and by going off with him.

Somehow she managed to convince CJ to let her help, but the task became a daunting one after Elizabeth surveyed CJ's available wardrobe of denim, denim and more denim. Elizabeth needed help and fast, so she swallowed her pride and called Hope Carrington. It was noon when the Lavender Hill Equestrian School's minivan pulled up to the cottage. Excited and optimistic, Elizabeth charged out to greet Hope.

"Thank you. Thank you. You are positively a lifesaver."

Hope looked understandably confused. "Just whose life am I saving?"

"Cole's. And CJ's. I have it on good authority that Alexandra and Mitzy Lexington are attending tonight and gunning for Cole. I'm nearly sure they're out to publicly embarrass him somehow and they won't mind a bit using his feelings for CJ to do it."

Hope frowned. "Why?"

Uh-oh. How do I explain the animosity and not lie? "Jason Lexington—Mitzy's son and Alexandra's brother—had some dealings with Cole. The Lexingtons packed Jason off to Europe to get him away from bad influences. Unfortunately, Jason's character ran true, and he indulged in all sorts of excesses before he killed himself speeding down a mountain road in France. The Lexingtons have held a grudge against Cole since then but have kept it quiet partially because Cole was away and also out of respect for Laurel Glen and your dad. But now, with Cole back and his practice and good reputation growing, the Lexingtons are ready to slice and dice him and anyone he cares about. Once they see him with CJ and the way he looks at her, they'll know how to get to Cole."

Hope frowned. "Why help CJ?"

"Because if Cole isn't in love with her, I'll eat my horse!" Elizabeth exclaimed. She paused, eyeing Hope. "Cole is my friend. Just as Jeff was. That's all either of them ever were. Cole's been using me as a shield."

A look of comprehension spread over Hope's face. "So his family wouldn't do exactly what you're about to?"

Elizabeth smiled. "Exactly."

Hope chuckled, and Elizabeth felt instant camaraderie with her.

"Let's go save my brother and cook his goose at the same time," Hope suggested. "I brought everything in my closet I thought would work on CJ."

After loading their arms with garments and bags of shoes and purses, the two mounted the porch and wrestled their loads into the little parlor.

"And now it begins," Hope said with a mischievous grin when everything was inside.

And it did. Several hours later Elizabeth gazed at their creation with pride and confidence. Not only would CJ not provide the Lexington women with ammunition, but her transformation was sure to push Cole over the edge into accepting his feelings.

CJ, however, still wasn't sure about any of it. "But how is looking like someone else going to make Cole admit he cares for me?" she asked, staring at the relative stranger in the mirror.

"You look beautiful," Hope told CJ. "And you don't look like someone else. You look as if you've tried to look your very best and succeeded."

"But this was so much trouble. And if he notices *this* person, and cares for *this* person, then he's noticing someone else and caring for someone else."

Hope huffed out a breath. "It took this same kind of makeover to get Jeff to stop seeing me as a little girl."

"And ask Hope what I looked like before my mother decided to find out if there was a way to improve on Mother Nature's unexplainable mistake," Elizabeth suggested, wishing her voice hadn't sounded so wistful. Wishing she'd been born even half as beautiful as her gorgeous mother and thinking about the unlikelihood that Jack would ever love the person inside Elizabeth.

Hope frowned at Elizabeth for a long moment. "You know, everyone is always talking about you before the metamorphosis, but I don't remember you as anything but a gorgeous butterfly."

Elizabeth felt her heart squeeze. If only that could be true. She forced a smile. "My old caterpillar self thanks you, my dear."

Hope continued to try convincing CJ that it was fine to fix herself up to attract a man.

"I can't say I don't like looking like this," CJ confided after a few minutes, "but it was so much trouble. Do you two actually go through all this? All the time?"

Elizabeth laughed along with Hope, but this time Elizabeth forced her laughter. She *did* work at her appearance this hard. She had to, or someone might see the ugliness beneath the surface.

Chapter Eight

At eight sharp on Saturday night, Jackson turned into the drive Elizabeth's directions indicated. He slowed his truck to a stop in the long twisting drive. The main house loomed ahead. House? he thought with a mix of derision and consternation. Calling the three-story brick and stone edifice a house was an understatement if there ever was one.

He tried not to feel intimidated but it was hard. He'd felt the same way when he'd first seen Laurel House, though since then the comfortable friendliness of his family's home had made it seem smaller and downright cozy. Looking through the trees at Elizabeth's parents' place, he felt as if he'd fallen down a rabbit hole and onto an old Hollywood set for a program like *Dynasty*. It was twice the size of Laurel House and not half as welcoming. He shook his head. Why would folks want to live in a museum of a home so big they couldn't find each other without a map?

Jackson blew out the breath he hadn't even realized had dammed up in his lungs. He refused to be cowed by the opulence. She might be a princess, and he was far from a prince, but he was also just as far from being a pauper. His family didn't display their assets as pretentiously as Elizabeth's did. That was all there was to it.

Knowing she waited got him moving again. Almost immediately the drive twisted left, and he realized the glint he'd seen when he entered the gate must have come from the diamond-patterned, leaded-glass windows he could see peeking over the hedge. He turned into the side drive as she'd told him to do and followed it around to a carriage house that was well hidden behind a row of tall boxwood and was partially covered in ivy. This was more like it. Homier. It was just as Elizabeth had described it.

He passed two arched carriage doors and turned again, finally coming to the side of the dwelling with a little arched window complete with flower-filled window box and a door of the same shape. Jackson couldn't shake the thought that any minute a troop of seven very short men would emerge and whistle their way off to work. Elizabeth's home looked as unreal as her parents' but it was like something out of a fairy tale rather than a Hollywood movie set.

"Jack," Elizabeth said a little breathlessly when she answered her door.

Dressed in a silvery white dress that fell to the floor, and wearing a diamond necklace, earrings and a bracelet that were probably worth what he'd paid for his truck, she was beautiful. She had a classic beauty that would only be more evident as the years marched on. Her hair, pulled from her face in twisting spirals and anchored high on either side of her head with silver combs, shone with sun-touched highlights even in dusk's low light. From the top of her head to the tip of her toes she was every inch a princess.

But he'd expected that.

What had him standing—staring—was the transcendent innocence that shone past all the careful artifice. It shocked him mute, like a revelation from above. Jackson finally understood what he'd been missing. Vulnerable, kind, loyal, she epitomized everything he'd ever been attracted to in a woman. But she was more.

Elizabeth was the end of his search for love.

And he realized something else, as well. This could be the most important night of his life. The beginning of a lifetime.

He swallowed with difficulty. "Maybe we should take your car," he said around the lump in his throat. "It just wouldn't be right to arrive with the most beautiful woman in Pennsylvania and hand her out of a pickup truck."

Elizabeth's smile was oddly shy, as if she didn't hear compliments such as that every day. She looked down and opened her little jeweled purse, taking out a set of keys.

"If you want to drive my car, Jack, just ask. You don't need to use flattery."

Rather than jump to the conclusion that she was

fishing for compliments, as he would have a few weeks ago, Jackson understood that for some reason Elizabeth didn't see what everyone else saw when she looked in a mirror. And most assuredly she didn't see what he saw.

The perfect woman for him.

Jackson stepped forward and kissed her cheek while palming the keys. "I hate your car, Elizabeth," he whispered near her ear. "It's an expensive tin can on wheels. I just think it fits a formal occasion more than my truck."

She stepped back and, wide-eyed, she stared at him. "I like your truck." Then she nodded toward the keys to her car. "I hope you don't mind a standard transmission too much," she said finally in a perplexed tone.

"Is there any other kind?" Jack asked and smiled when she finally did.

During the half hour drive Elizabeth filled him in on the punishing race that was to take place the next day. She also explained why it had caused the rift to widen between Cole and Ross Taggert. It was a tragic story. Ross's first wife had been killed riding a horse to show Cole that Ross was right and fifteen-year-old Cole had nothing to fear. But it had been Cole who was right, and he'd watched his mother be trampled before Ross could put the horse down. Cole, Elizabeth said, had not been the same since, nor had his relationship with Ross.

They arrived at Graystone Manor and, following her instructions, Jackson showed his invitation to a tuxedo-clad guard at an imposing iron gate set into an equally daunting fifteen-foot stone wall. The guard nodded and handed back the invitation.

"Am I done with this?" he asked Elizabeth as he eased off the clutch and put the car in first gear.

She shook her head. "We'll need it at the door. Charles Graystone likes his security tight. He doesn't need it but it makes him feel important."

Jackson drove onto the estate, past lush gardens, and pulled to a stop before stone steps. They'd clearly had been designed to be intimidating rather than inviting. Compared to Graystone Manor, Elizabeth's parents' mansion and Laurel House looked like starter houses.

The house was built of stone, like the surrounding high walls and imposing stairs. It had massive towers, parapets and, as if to add a truly macabre air, there were gargoyles aplenty. It defied comment. At least until Elizabeth let out an unladylike snort.

Her tone thick with sarcasm she said, "Welcome to Graystone. Home of Chester County's Gothic Nightmare. Halloween would be so much more appropriate a night for their annual show-off-the-homestead affair, don't you think?"

Jackson chuckled. "I met one of their daughters when I taught the kids at Jeff's camp how to barrel race. She seems like a nice girl." He shook his head in disbelief. "I can't believe they actually have children living in that…that—"

"Monstrosity?" Elizabeth asked. "Those poor girls. Several years ago they had to rent out a local restaurant because little Natalie's friends were afraid to come here for her birthday party.''

Jackson shook his head in disgust and climbed out of Elizabeth's high-priced tin can. When a valet appeared, he tossed the youth the keys. ''Don't bury it too deep, buddy. It may be a short night.''

''Why did you say that?'' Elizabeth asked as they climbed the steps to the front door.

He took her hand and entwined her arm with his against his side. ''Because if you keep making comments like that, we'll get tossed out of here within the hour.''

She patted his forearm. ''Relax. I'm nothing if not diplomatic.''

But he noticed minutes later that it was Elizabeth who'd grown tense. In retrospect, Jackson realized she'd been a little edgy since she'd opened her door. He'd been hoping it wasn't him that made her tense, but it had gotten much worse since they'd strolled into the main area where most people had gathered. ''Is something wrong?'' he asked, feeling the tautness in the muscles of her arm.

''Remember the piranha I told you about? The ones always looking for ways to make Cole's life difficult?''

''I thought you knew they'd be here.''

She nodded. ''I did, but I didn't tell you they aren't very nice to me, either.''

''That makes sense, in a way, since you're Cole's friend. Well, don't worry. I have thick skin if they try picking on me.''

* * *

Elizabeth didn't correct Jack or tell him it wasn't his skin but his opinion of her she was afraid would suffer. As much as she wanted to spend time with Jack, she knew she'd never have agreed to this date if she hadn't had the added incentive of feeling duty bound to try to protect CJ. After all, CJ and Cole were targets because of Elizabeth.

Minutes later, Elizabeth realized she was holding her breath as she and Jack passed in front of Alexandra and Mitzy Lexington.

She had begun to think she'd gotten away scot-free when she heard Mitzy say, "Apparently Elizabeth is at it again—yet another conquest. I wonder how long he'll last." Her sigh was theatrical. "They never stay once they find out what she's really like."

Jack stiffened.

"We should warn him, don't you think, Alex dear?" Mitzy went on in a voice Elizabeth knew was loud enough for Jack to hear. "I understand he calls himself a Christian. He should know about how she entices men and just how young she started practicing on the unsuspecting—corrupting them with her wiles."

Elizabeth thought she'd die when Jack stopped and turned to face the two women. "The name's Jack Alton. And you are?"

Mitzy was even more taken aback than Elizabeth that Jack would directly confront them.

"Uh, I am Alexandra Lexington and this is my mother, Mitzy," the younger of the two said, gesturing to the middle-aged viper who'd spoken in the stage whisper and who stood gaping at Jack.

"Ladies, you're right. I am a Christian, and the Lord demands of me that I act with kindness at all times. Right now, I'm tempted to disobey Him but—" He stopped, the line of his jaw as hard as granite. "Jesus once said, 'He who is without sin, cast the first stone.' Think about it." He turned to Elizabeth.

Elizabeth let him lead her away. He looked so annoyed and handsome in his tux. His deeply tanned skin was just a little higher in color now, betraying how much he probably wanted to say more. But he needn't bother. She'd never seen those two so beautifully put in their places. All she could do was stare at him, trying for all the world to abolish the vision of him galloping toward her in gleaming armor on the back of a huge warhorse.

"Close your mouth, darlin'. You look like a fish. A beautiful, elegant fish, but a fish nonetheless."

"But—but don't you want to know?"

"Know?" he asked, as if he couldn't imagine what he'd ask.

"What they meant. Don't you want to know what they meant?"

"Those two?" He shot her a look that asked after her sanity. "Of course I don't. If I've given you the impression I would, I'm sorry. I was jealous. I wanted you on my arm, and you seemed to be involved with my, ah, with my boss's son. Tonight you're with me. I've got no complaints."

"Oh." She blinked, unsure if she should believe

him. Was this man real? He seemed to mean what he said, if the earnest expression he wore was anything to go by.

"Would you like to dance?" Jack asked.

Dance? She couldn't dance with him. It had been the heat of his body that had triggered her fear the day he'd kissed her. What if it happened again in the middle of all these people? When she'd accepted his invitation, she hadn't thought he would ask this of her. She'd heard devout Christians didn't dance. His church has a rock band for worship, Elizabeth. What were you thinking?

She looked into Jack's beautiful eyes and wanted more than anything to be normal for just one night. She wanted to make a grab for the brass ring. She wanted to be able to let this man hold her. She wanted to feel safer in his arms than she'd felt since the day she'd learned to fear men.

"Okay," she replied, forcing herself to smile while she fought inner panic.

He answered with a warm smile of his own and directed her toward the orchestra. At the edge of the marble dance floor, he took her in his arms. She was suddenly Cinderella at the ball.

And all her dreams—good and bad—came true because her prince was a good dancer. She was not. Like the storybook heroine, Elizabeth didn't dance— out of necessity rather than lack of opportunity.

She had danced a few times with Cole and Jeff. She felt safe with them, seeing them more in the role of dutiful brothers than dates. Her father had also partnered with her when her role of daughter demanded it. She could usually pull it off quite nicely by concentrating on where she put her feet.

Tonight, though, Jack's nearness proved a huge distraction, and her lack of dancing experience quickly showed itself. She winced yet again when she stepped on the toes of his gleaming black cowboy boots for the third time. "I'm sorry."

He sighed. "I wish being with me didn't make you so tense," he said, real regret in his voice.

He knew. She wanted to die. "No. I'm clumsy. That's all."

They came to the edge of the dance floor, and he dropped his arms. "I wasn't born yesterday, Elizabeth. I know something's wrong. What have I done to make you so jumpy?"

She reached out and grasped his forearm. The muscle beneath her fingers was strong and steady, but she knew he'd never use that strength to hurt her. How could she tell him it wasn't a bad kind of nervousness distracting her?

"No. It's me," she said instead. "I wish I could—"

"Elizabeth," a stern voice said from behind.

Her father. Elizabeth's heart fell. Not now.

She turned to face Reginald Boyer, and her consternation doubled. Her mother stood at her father's side looking all pinch-mouthed and annoyed. She'd told them she wouldn't be going to the Graystone Ball and hadn't thought to let them know her plans had changed. Thank goodness they'd never lower themselves to argue in public.

"Mother. Father. I'd like you to meet my escort for the evening, Jack Alton. Jack, my father, Reginald Boyer."

"Taggert's new number-two man?" her father asked but didn't take Jack's hand. The frown stayed in place.

"Yes, sir. I signed on as Laurel Glen's foreman just before the West Nile problem," Jack said and looked at his extended hand, practically forcing her father to shake it. Which, after shooting a furious glance at Elizabeth, her father did, but with little grace.

"And this is my mother, Louise," Elizabeth said, hoping her lack of enthusiasm didn't show.

"Alton. Alton? Of the West Chester Altons?"

"Colorado, ma'am."

"Oh," Elizabeth's mother replied with a look on her face that spoke of a bad smell. "I'd like a word with you, Elizabeth."

Elizabeth knew the problem. Jack didn't come with an Ivy League pedigree and more than likely didn't have the kind of bank account that could get them out of trouble. Lance Goodwin Bond had both, and she'd refused to attend the Graystone Ball with him. Of course, she would have refused to attend a dog-fight with that pompous jerk. Consequently her parents saw her as an ungrateful daughter, and she was sure they'd cast Jack in the part of interloper.

Just then she caught the look that passed between

her parents. There was no way she was leaving Jack with her father, and besides, she and her mother had talked enough lately. Especially since Louise Boyer had developed a one-track mind—and that track was named Lance!

Threading her arm with Jack's, Elizabeth replied, "I don't think so, Mother. Perhaps I'll see you after the event tomorrow. Jack, darling," she continued, pretending not to notice her mother's glare. "I think I heard something about a cold supper in the dining room. Shall we see what there is to offer?"

"Perhaps you're right," her father snapped. "But we *will* talk tomorrow."

"What was that all about?" Jack asked.

"Some mothers dream of a knight in shining armor for their daughter. My mother dreamed of a nice fat bank account with legs. She's a little miffed that I wouldn't come here with a certain prime specimen after all the work she went to reeling him in."

After all, Elizabeth thought, what did her mother care if her daughter was happy as long as she secured a new source of funds—one with an acceptable pedigree—for their life-style?

They were almost out of the conservatory, where the orchestra had begun a series of melancholy show tunes, when they came upon Cole standing apart from his family. He didn't see them but looked longingly toward where the Taggerts stood talking with CJ Larson.

"So what do you think of CJ's new look?" Elizabeth asked from behind him.

Cole pivoted to face her and Jack Alton. "What did you have to do with this? CJ never dresses like that."

Elizabeth held up her hand, suddenly fighting a smile. Cole was down for the count. "It's Hope's dress and shoes. All I did was stop by to make sure CJ didn't embarrass you tonight."

"I'd never be embarrassed by CJ," Cole snapped.

Elizabeth arched her brow and adopted the persona of the idle rich she often taunted Cole with. "Believe me, you would have died rather than walk in here with her dressed in a pair of velvet jeans and a silk shirt."

Cole gritted his teeth. "I wouldn't have cared. It might have made tonight easier. Did you ever think of that?" He didn't wait for a reply but stalked away.

Elizabeth chuckled, sure the look she shot him was all the answer he needed to decipher her twofold mission. The Lexingtons would have torn CJ apart had Elizabeth and Hope not acted, and it was an added bonus that Cole would have a hard time resisting CJ's obvious charms.

"I don't get you two. Why was he so mad and why were you so—"

"Difficult? You have a sister, right? Try using the same frame of reference for me and Cole."

Elizabeth watched Jack's eyes go from confused to thoughtful, a little smile tipping his lips. Suddenly he made sense to her. He really was jealous of Cole. She hadn't believed it when he'd confessed earlier. For a second she felt all the feminine power she'd ever dreamed of possessing. But reality quickly intruded. She had no idea what to do with such power, and the thought of trying to use it terrified her.

Chapter Nine

Jackson stared ahead, trying on Elizabeth's suggestion for size. His sister, Crystal, was his best friend, and though no one knew it but a few close family members, they weren't any more related than Elizabeth and Cole. Crystal and Jackson had also developed a weird kind of silent communication, and it often took only a look to know what the other was thinking. And that was what Elizabeth was trying to tell him. It was what she'd already told him last Sunday at church. He let it sink in. Cole had never stood between them. Jackson's imagination had.

He looked across the dance floor as Cole asked a gorgeous blonde to dance. "Don't look now but I think your plan just backfired."

Elizabeth giggled. "No, it didn't. That is CJ Larson."

After recovering from the shock of hearing Elizabeth Boyer giggle, Jackson blinked and looked again.

Sure enough… "No way. Oh, Cole's a goner," he pronounced after identifying the trainer's features. He turned to Elizabeth and felt as if his heart were being squeezed in a vise. Her eyes were alight with mischief, and her smile gleamed wide and undisguised. He felt love for her swell inside him till he thought he would burst.

Then he caught sight of the forbidding figures of Reginald and Louise Boyer standing in the doorway and his joy evaporated. Her parents were going to be a problem. They were clearly livid that he was with their daughter. She didn't seem to care, but how could that be? He remembered what Meg had said about the couple as parents and what Elizabeth had said about trying to adjust to being considered a failure by her mother. Would Elizabeth continue to defy them or eventually seek their favor?

Tonight it didn't seem to matter, Jackson realized. If heartbreak lay ahead, then he might as well steam on toward it because when Elizabeth opened her door earlier tonight, she'd sealed his destiny.

He knew the second her parents spotted them and moved forward. Jackson decided to put off another confrontation. "You know what? I could use some air and I'd like to get a closer look at those gardens we saw on the way up the drive. They almost make up for the haunted castle atmosphere."

"Through there," she said, pointing toward an open doorway. They walked down a wide hall lined with huge portraits of men and women he assumed were Graystone ancestors, then entered another conservatory that led to the garden. The well-lit, perfectly engineered copy of a formal English garden added to the feeling Jackson had when they'd pulled up in front of the mansion, as if he'd been transported an ocean away. Had this been a tourist attraction or a theme park, he probably would have thought the effect interesting and enjoyed it. But this was supposed to be a family home. And a less homey place he'd never seen.

"Didn't this Graystone fella ever hear we fought a war to kick out the British and their class system with them?"

Elizabeth laughed, a china bell sound that gladdened Jackson's heart.

"Don't fool yourself about the class system. It's alive and well almost everywhere old money still exists. But that's what I like most about you, Jack. You aren't impressed by all this. The funniest thing of all is that Graystone isn't old money. He's just trying desperately to blend in with it. Those ancestors we just passed in his gallery were bought and paid for. His wife goes to estate auctions all the time and buys old portraits the real descendants don't want any more. Sort of retro adoption."

Jackson stopped next to a fountain and studied her in the glow of the underwater lights. "You're pulling my chain. Right?"

Elizabeth grinned and shook her head. "Sorry."

"Please tell me most of those people in there aren't impressed by all this."

"I'm sure Ross Taggert and his entire clan are

laughing up their collective sleeves. They've stayed away before. They're only here because Ross is riding in the Graystone Cross-country tomorrow."

"I hope he's right and it helps business. I looked at some old records, and the farm hasn't bounced back all the way after the trouble they had last summer."

"It should help. A lot of people who should have remained loyal to Laurel Glen didn't. Most made promises about returning their stock once the vandal was caught, but so far only half have."

"You know what's odd? I was looking at a book Amelia did on the original residents of Chester County, and the Taggerts are an original land grant family. The oldest of the old money, and they are the least affected by it."

"They've stayed in the business end of their farm and they've added to their holdings over generations. In other words, they haven't always been as successful as they are now. They aren't strangers to adversity, either. Ross's father died very young and didn't have his financial ducks in a row. I understand from Cole that it was part miracle and the rest hard work for Ross to manage to hold on to the place. That's why he's so willing to run in the cross-country tomorrow. He worked hard to make a success of Laurel Glen and he's determined to be on top again the way he was before Harry Donovan started causing trouble last summer."

"So why are you here?"

She smiled shyly. "Besides that you asked me?"

He grinned, loving the happy sparkle in her eyes. "Yeah. Besides that."

"I usually come for the chance to pick up a patron or two for New Life Inn. This year Charles Graystone is donating a percentage of the gate to us. As for why the others came…" She shrugged. "I couldn't say. I just know all this stopped impressing me a long time ago."

"Why? You were raised in this world."

Jackson was horrified to see tears well in her eyes. "Because there are things more important than money and status. A lot of those people in there don't understand that."

He had a feeling she counted her parents among those people. She suddenly looked sad, and her eyes took on an unfocused look that was filled with pain and anguish and something more worrisome that he couldn't decipher. Wanting to comfort her, he caressed her cheek and enfolded her in his arms.

She looked up, her lashes spiky with unshed tears, and he dipped his head, kissing her forehead, her temples, her soft cheek, then those tempting lips. The woman had him bewitched, Jackson thought as he deepened the kiss and pulled her closer.

"No!" she gasped, shoving him as she backed away.

"What?" His head swimming in confusion, Jackson just barely caught himself before he tumbled into the fountain.

"I can't," she whispered, shakily. "I'm sorry. I wish I could be different but I can't—"

"Fine!" Jackson snapped. He got the message. She might know there were things more important than money and status but she couldn't let go of the world to which she was born. He'd heard it all before. He wasn't part of Colorado's high society, either, no matter how much the Circle A was worth.

"I'm sorry," she whispered.

"No, don't apologize. Better I get the message now. I don't fit in your world. The valet has your keys. Why don't you take care of business for your women's shelter and I'll hop a ride with someone else. I imagine one of the Taggerts will give me a lift home. Have a nice life with your well-heeled friends, Elizabeth."

He turned and walked off, hoping he didn't get so lost inside he'd have to ask any of these pretentious fools for a map.

Meg Taggert saw Elizabeth rush across the foyer toward the front door. Her young friend looked devastated and was clearly fighting tears. Meg caught her by the arm. "What is it, dear? What's wrong?"

"Me. I'm wrong," Elizabeth said, her voice betraying a soul-deep anguish. "But Jack doesn't understand. And why should he even try? Why should any man put up with me? I should just make up my mind to be alone. That way nobody gets hurt. I didn't mean to hurt him." She sniffled and looked over Meg's shoulder. "I have to go. I think I'll sleep in tomorrow, after all. Maybe I'll see you at the cross-country."

She turned and hurried away before Meg could ask another question. More than not knowing what had gone wrong, it bothered her that Elizabeth had canceled their church plans just when she needed the Lord most. She sighed. Young people. They never looked in the right place for answers.

"Was that Elizabeth?" Louise Boyer asked. Meg had been so deeply engrossed in her thoughts that she hadn't heard anyone approach.

Meg suddenly understood what had caused Elizabeth to turn and leave so abruptly. It was sad. Most young women ran to their mothers, but Elizabeth found it necessary to flee hers. "I believe she remembered somewhere else she needed to be," Meg answered truthfully, not adding, "Anywhere where you weren't," even though she was dying to put this woman in her place.

"Well, I'm thankful for small favors. Imagine her accepting an invitation from a farmworker. Hopefully she came to her senses."

"She seemed a bit upset," Meg told the odious woman.

"She more than likely saw how badly he fit in with our set. Why, he could barely lead her around the floor for a simple dance."

Meg ground her teeth wondering how long she could keep silent. "Actually, I danced with Jack just a few minutes ago. He dances divinely, though he did seem a bit grim."

"I don't care if his heart is bleeding all over his

rented tux. He should have known his place and not asked my daughter to come here with him.''

"Jack is a wonderful young man. Conscientious. Hardworking. Godly. She could do a lot worse.''

"And she could do much better. I still can't believe she turned down Lance Goodwin Bond to come here with that common man.''

Meg itched to list more of her son's assets, especially the size and wealth of the Circle A—the only thing that would be important to Louise Boyer—but she resisted. Instead she said, "We all have our priorities, Louise. I've always known ours were different but I never realized they were polar opposites. I really must go.''

Meg went to look for Jackson to find out what in the world Elizabeth had been talking about. Unfortunately, she learned he'd left with Ross and Amelia, whose baby was due in a couple weeks. Hope and Jeff were following, so Meg set out for home. She turned at the front door, looked at the magnificently terrible house and vowed never to set eyes on it again.

Meg was up bright and early the next morning and found Jackson on the front porch of the foreman's cottage nursing a cup of coffee and staring into space.

"You look as if you've lost your last friend, son.''

"Actually it was one I guess I never had,'' he replied. "I'm tired of being disappointed in people, you know.''

"And hurt by people? One young lady in particular?''

"Elizabeth Boyer is no different than any of the rest. I speculate that it's some weird gene passed to me that makes me seek out women who think I'm some sort of walk on the wild side, but then they turn around and head back where they came from, to a world I don't even want to deal with."

Meg raised an eyebrow and leaned over the porch rail. "That made about as much sense as what Elizabeth said last night."

That perked him right up. "You talked to Elizabeth last night?"

Meg walked onto the porch and sat in the rocker next to her son. "Just before she left. You know, when I gave you into the Altons' care, I assumed one of the many lessons they'd teach you is that you don't take a young woman somewhere then leave her to her own devices."

"It was her car. I was the one looking for a ride home."

"She was in tears, Jack. I expected better of you and I told you she's a lot more fragile than she appears."

"So she blamed me?"

"On the contrary. She blamed herself."

"And she should. She's also every bit as snobby and class-conscious as her parents. Except she told me she thinks judging people by their bank balance and lineage is wrong. So she knows they're wrong and doesn't have the strength to go against them. She allows herself little rebellions but she'll only go so far."

"Told you all that, did she?"

Jack frowned even more. "Well, no. But she nearly shoved me in a fountain because I kissed her."

"And *that* tells you she thinks you aren't good enough for her?" Meg shook her head. "She said you didn't understand, and it appears you don't."

"She acted as if she were afraid I'd contaminate her." Jack stormed, clearly insulted.

Meg might have smiled if the picture of Elizabeth she'd been building in her mind hadn't just had the color of fear added to it, turning it a little ugly and tragic.

"I think you better think about her reaction. And ask yourself why you jumped to the conclusion that she was rejecting you because of your social status and not for something she has no control over. I saw a heartbroken young lady last night who was worried she'd hurt you, and not one who cast off an inconvenience."

Jack didn't even hear his mother leave because he was so deep in thought. He looked up, and she'd melted away almost as if she hadn't been there offering him advice. He forced himself to think about why he'd thought Elizabeth was rejecting him because of her parents. And he didn't like the conclusion he came to. He was giving the motives of the women in his past to Elizabeth. He'd certainly gotten angry enough when he'd thought she was judging him on the actions of his predecessor at Laurel Glen. But all she had really done was apologize.

I can't. I'm sorry. I wish I could be different but I can't—

Maybe he should have asked what she'd been about to say instead of jumping in to prevent what he'd judged would be hurtful words. Maybe he should ask now.

He looked at his watch. He was supposed to transport Ross's Prize, the big stallion Ross would ride in the Graystone Cross-country, to the event grounds. He'd take a look around to see if she was there.

And ask her what he should have asked last night.

Chapter Ten

Elizabeth watched in shock as the helicopter bearing Ross Taggert lifted off from the Graystone Cross-country's temporary helipad. This couldn't be good, she thought. She had no idea what was wrong, but they didn't airlift patients who weren't seriously ill.

The odd thing was that she'd heard CJ's name announced as the rider from Laurel Glen. She was, in fact, riding in Ross's place at that very moment, so there was no way he'd gotten hurt in the cross-country event.

Elizabeth felt as if one of her family had been felled. She'd gone to the Graystone event with half a heart, really wanting to stay in bed and brood about Jack. Maybe dream about him, since dreams were all she'd ever have. But Charles Graystone had promised a portion of the proceeds this year to the New Life Inn, so she felt obligated. Having seen the look of anguish on Cole's face as the helicopter rotated and sped off, her problems should seem unimportant. Instead, the whole worrisome incident added to her melancholy state.

If God didn't keep Ross, who was important to so many of His followers, safe, then He'd never help her. Dispirited and confused, Elizabeth felt a hand on her shoulder.

She turned. It was her father.

"They were arguing again. Cole was screaming at Ross for letting CJ ride the course. Ross just crumpled. I was up on the press platform above them."

"Do you know what's wrong?"

Reginald Boyer shook his head. "I don't like the man, but I don't wish him any ill. And Cole's such a bleeding heart, he'll never stop blaming himself if something happens to that stubborn father of his."

Elizabeth glanced toward the medical tent and saw one of the medics on his way inside. He was the same man who had helped load Ross into the helicopter. She started moving toward the makeshift infirmary before the idea of asking questions fully formed in her brain. "I'm going to see what I can find out," she told her father.

"Excuse me," she said to the medic as she followed him out of the stifling August heat a few minutes later. "Can you tell me what's wrong with Ross Taggert?"

He shook his head. "I'm sorry, miss. I'm not at liberty to say."

"Do you know where they took him?"

The medic named the biggest—not closest—hospital in the area, which meant they thought he needed specialized care. And quickly. It was serious, but that wasn't new information. The use of a helicopter had told her that. Maybe, though, everyone had over-reacted.

"Please. I need more information. I'm a close friend of Mr. Taggert's. I need to call the rest of the family. Please."

The tall, thin man looked around the empty tent and sighed. "His son, the vet, thinks Taggert had a stroke, but we thought heat exhaustion since there's been a lot of that today. Could be both, though. But you didn't hear it from me. Okay?"

She nodded. "Thank you so much," Elizabeth said. "Mind if I call the family from in here? I don't think this is the kind of news they need to get with a lot of merriment in the background."

Elizabeth made the call but learned from the house-keeper that Cole had contacted the family already and they were on their way to the hospital. Next she needed to find CJ. Cole would need her, especially if he was blaming himself. She turned to rush out but crashed into Jack on his way into the tent.

"Elizabeth! Do you know what happened to Ross?" he demanded, grabbing her elbows and steadying her. His hands and his voice shook, and there was a lot more than mild concern for an employer in his eyes. She wondered at that, but her mind veered at the feel of him so near.

His tight grip should have frightened her, but instead it made her concern for him deepen. He didn't let go immediately. Instead, he held on to her as if she were a lifeline.

Her mind relived that scene in the garden once again. If only she hadn't pushed him away. If only he hadn't misunderstood. The idea of her rejecting him because of her parents' wishes was ludicrous in the extreme. Still, though she longed to explain, she saw no sense in trying. What could she say, after all? She couldn't come right out and tell him she'd been stupid and had trusted the wrong person. That as a result she'd been raped. That she would never have a normal relationship with a man. That even after all the years that had passed since that day, she still flashed back to the feeling of being powerless in a man's arms. That even Jack, a man she longed to hold, would never be able to hold her in return without fear stealing her joy—and his.

She was damaged. Flawed. And there was no future for them.

But there were other people they both cared about. It was time to focus on them. So she motioned Jack outside the tent to a crude bench in the shade of a tree. She quickly filled him in on what she'd learned, which felt like very little.

"I feel so responsible," Jack said when she'd finished. "When I found out CJ was riding the cross-country for him, I called Ross to see how he was feeling. He said he had a miserable headache but he about had a cow when I mentioned that CJ planned to ride in his place. It upset him. He'd been going to scratch Prize after walking the course because it was so dangerous, but his head felt so bad he didn't bother telling CJ.''

Jack wiped the sweat from his forehead. "He said he'd be back as soon as he could get here. I was supposed to find CJ and stop her. Maybe if he'd stayed home, he might not be on his way to the hospital right now.''

"Now isn't the time for self-recriminations, Jack. You didn't call to upset him or to get him to come back here. You were just concerned. I assume you never found CJ since she did ride for him.''

Jack grabbed the back of his neck and stood, pacing away a couple steps and then back. "I was at Prize's trailer looking for her when I heard her announced as the Laurel Glen rider. That's why I wasn't at the start line when Ross collapsed. I hoofed it back there but only in time to find out who'd been in the chopper I'd seen overhead.''

"We need to find CJ and send her to the hospital,'' Elizabeth said. "Cole's going to be a mess over this, especially if he and Ross were arguing.''

"Okay, but after that I'd like us to have a long talk.''

Elizabeth nodded and stood. She couldn't imagine what he wanted to talk about. Last night he'd wished her a good life and walked out of it. What more was there to say?

The crowded grounds made finding CJ difficult. They missed her at the finish line, so they went to the trailer. Neither she nor the horse was there, and Jackson worried that the stallion had been injured. They headed to the vet tent. There they learned that one of the vets on duty had stopped CJ on her way to the trailer to take a look at the horse just as a precaution. They realized that was why she and the stallion hadn't been at the trailer.

They approached the green and gold Laurel Glen trailer again and saw Prize tethered to the back. Elizabeth called CJ's name. CJ had just pushed herself to her feet when they walked around the front of the trailer. She looked a little groggy, as if she'd been napping. The news of Ross Taggert's sudden illness clearly had not reached her.

"I know. I know. Riding for Ross was a little out there. Actually, considering the course, it was a *lot* out there, but—"

"CJ," Elizabeth interrupted. "Didn't you hear? Ross collapsed right after you started the course. They used the standby helicopter and flew him to the hospital. Cole went with him."

CJ paled beneath her healthy tan and dropped onto the chrome running board of the pickup. She confirmed that Ross had only told her about his headache and his plans to go home.

"Well, he came back," Elizabeth told her. "From what I hear, he collapsed near the start line right after you took off. My father says he thinks Ross and Cole were arguing."

"All those two ever do is argue," Jackson grumbled, knowing he and his father were not much better. Elizabeth took CJ's hand and gave her the keys to her car. "Take my car and go. Cole will need you there."

Shaking her head, CJ stood and handed the keys back. Which could only mean CJ and Cole were still dancing around one another. Didn't they know how lucky they were? Didn't they know what they were giving up? Didn't they know that Jackson would give his left arm to have with Elizabeth what those two clearly had together?

"You take these back and get yourself to that hospital," Elizabeth ordered, plunking the keys into CJ's hand again. "My car is at the entrance to the trailer lot."

CJ looked at the keys. "All right," she conceded.

Anxiously Jackson watched Elizabeth stare after CJ, her mind lost somewhere unreachable. Her look of longing tugged at his heartstrings.

"So, you need a lift home?" Jackson asked, hopeful his show of temper last night hadn't put her off permanently. Hopeful he'd misread her rejection.

"I should stay since the New Life Inn is a beneficiary," Elizabeth said, "but after hearing CJ's opinion of the course and seeing all the trouble this event has caused, I just don't think I can."

"Then suppose I get Prize loaded. We'll drop him at Laurel Glen and I'll check on a few things. Then I'll take you home or to the hospital. Whichever you want. But first I want to apologize for—"

"No. Please," she cut in. "It was my fault. I shouldn't have reacted the way I did."

"And maybe I should have asked what was wrong

instead of assuming. There's an old saying about assuming that I forgot.''

Jackson watched a little smile tip Elizabeth's lips up at the corners, but then she grew serious again. ''I really don't care what my parents think, you know. That wasn't the problem.''

''Mind telling me what was?''

Elizabeth shook her head. ''I can't. I just can't.'' She squeezed her eyes shut but not before he glimpsed a soul-deep anguish reflected in them. Twin tears tracked down her cheeks, and she looked at him. ''You were right last night. You're better off without me. I'm just not worth all the turmoil. As you said, have a nice life, Jack.''

If Jackson hadn't liked thinking she'd pushed him away because of her parents' disapproval, he really didn't like what he was thinking now. Seeing now. But with his mother's warning that Elizabeth was emotionally fragile and with so many other little clues screaming in his mind, he could no longer deny that it all pointed to Elizabeth having been ill-used by some man. Jackson wasn't sure how, and he couldn't even bring himself to speculate. All he could do was love her, earn her trust and pray for self-control when he finally did learn the whole story. Because right then he wanted to demand names and go break a few heads. Not a very Christian attitude, but there it was. He'd never felt such anger and anguish at the same time.

She turned and tried to flee.

Jackson put a hand on her shoulder to stop her.

''Beth, you don't really want to go, do you?'' he asked and turned her into his arms. Remembering her reaction last night when he'd tightened his embrace, he kept his arms looped as gently around her as he could while still keeping her sheltered.

Soon he realized she was crying. She didn't make a sound, but her tears soaked his shirt. There was something poignant in those silent tears that tore at him. Had she been fighting this battle alone? Had no one ever heard her cry for compassion?

Thinking of her parents, he knew they certainly hadn't. Perhaps his cousin had. Cole was certainly protective of her, and even though he might know what had happened in her past, there was no way Jackson could ask him. Elizabeth had to be the one to confide in him. And he had to show her he could be trusted.

He closed his eyes and held her with her head tucked under his chin, praying for wisdom and patience. He prayed that the Lord would touch her soul and heal whatever hurt kept her so isolated and afraid, for now he understood. Fear and a feeling of near worthlessness haunted Elizabeth.

His father had always told him that anything worth having was worth the work it took to get it, and Jackson knew gaining Elizabeth's trust wouldn't be easy. But he wanted this woman in his life, and that was worth any amount of hard work.

With God's help he would succeed.

Chapter Eleven

Jackson woke the morning after the Graystone Cross-country to find a new world outside his window. Overnight a wild line of thunderstorms had raced through southern Pennsylvania and Delaware bringing cool temperatures. The air seemed to have been freshly scrubbed, and the mercury had fallen at least thirty degrees from the ninety-nine of the day before. The humidity that had lain like a blanket over the land had lifted, as well.

The events of the night before raced through his mind. Ross was going to be all right, having suffered only a mild stroke. With very little therapy, and if he took the blood-pressure medicine he'd been ignoring, the doctors promised he'd be good as new within a month or two. But the night's excitement hadn't ended there.

A few minutes ago his mother had called to say that Ross's wife, Amelia delivered a baby girl sometime during the night. When the last rider finished his run in the late afternoon, it turned out that CJ had won the Graystone Cross-country, cheering Ross even more. And the best news from Jackson's point of view was that when he and Elizabeth had stopped by the hospital, it had been clear that CJ and Cole had settled whatever differences they'd had and appeared to be inseparable.

Elizabeth was still a worry, though. She'd been quiet after expressing her sympathy for Ross's unexpected illness. She'd smiled happily at Cole and CJ, giving what anyone could see was her stamp of approval on the match. She'd expressed her good wishes and her prayers for Amelia and the baby.

He'd left her then to see Ross, wanting to make sure his uncle knew Jackson would keep everything running smoothly at Laurel Glen. During his short visit with Ross, Elizabeth had taken her car and left.

And that was his worry. He didn't have a clue where her sudden departure left them. Recognizing the futility of his thoughts, he bounded out of bed. The day awaited, and brooding about what it would bring would accomplish nothing.

Several hours later, his mind once again on Elizabeth, a noise in the stable drew his attention. As if thinking about her had conjured her from thin air, she walked toward the door of his office. He stood. ''Well, hi. You left without saying goodbye.''

''I didn't really belong there.''

''That isn't the way Hope and Jeff or CJ and Cole

felt. Meg was pretty annoyed, too, when she came out of the labor room and found you'd gone.''

''Oh, no. Meg's been good to me. I guess I should have stayed till she and Hope switched as Amelia's labor coaches.''

Jackson willed Elizabeth to look him in the eye. Something, he realized minutes ago, she rarely did. ''I would have liked to come back to find you still there, as well.''

''Sorry. I thought it was time I left and I thought you'd be leaving, too, since you aren't family, either.''

Jackson was torn, and glad she was busy taking in the room and avoiding eye contact. He'd learned over the years that he wasn't a very convincing liar. And it felt uncomfortable—since he couldn't correct her misconception.

Meg was still unsure when to introduce him as her son. She didn't want to intrude on the joy Ross and Amelia's and Hope and Jeff's new additions brought to both couples by introducing her own one-hundred-and-ninety-pound bouncing baby boy to the family. He suspected she was wrestling with other issues, too. But whatever her reasons, until she broke her silence on the matter, Jackson's hands were tied. He couldn't be the one to give away her secret, even to Elizabeth. It wouldn't be right.

He wished it didn't feel so much like he was lying. ''I did leave right after you,'' he admitted and sat to cover his nervousness, ''but I'd hoped you'd have dinner with me.''

She smiled and looked toward the window over his shoulder, not meeting his eyes. "How about lunch today?" she asked.

"I'd love to. Unfortunately, I gave the summer kids an hour off. They wanted to go buy a gift for baby Laurel." He chuckled. "The boys wanted to buy her inline skates and the girls wanted a little T-shirt of some rock band."

"Teenagers aren't known for their practicality, I guess."

"Still, they're a good bunch. I'll be sorry to see them go back to school next month. Remember when you were their age?"

Elizabeth looked sad suddenly then grimaced as she sank into the chair facing him on the other side of his desk. "I was never their age. Not really," she said gravely.

"Tough teenage years? I pictured you as every teenage boy's fantasy come to life. You sure must have been mine."

"Only if you were into nightmares. I'd show you a picture but they never took pictures of me." She pulled a face. "Afraid I'd break the camera, probably. They didn't even bother buying those terrible ones the school took every year. My mother often refers to me in my early years as the Boyer family's ugly duckling. And I was, at least up until my mother plucked all my gray feathers and turned me into a swan."

Once again Jackson was tempted to take on her parents on her behalf. Some people shouldn't be parents. The Boyers were two of them. Jack forced a smile rather than grind his teeth, trying to remember that it was his duty to be forgiving. He wasn't there yet, however.

''If you turned into a swan, it's because that's what you were meant to be. And as for youthful fantasies, mine were more on the line of a girl who wasn't afraid of horses. My life has always revolved around them in one way or another. The Circle A is a cattle ranch, and a lot of work still gets done from the back of a horse. One of the things my father and I differ on is that I think half the operation should be geared toward an equine breeding program, since beef is getting such a bad name these days. He won't listen, though.''

''Maybe not listening to children happens genetically when people have them.''

Jack thought of Meg and the way she listened to him. She'd never known him as a child. Maybe that was the key. ''I wonder if it isn't just that parents always think of their children as the little ones they had to guide and protect. To them we never really grow up.''

Elizabeth grimaced. ''For some parents that's probably it. Others just want their children to be clones of them. It's what my parents want. It drove my brother away years ago.''

''I didn't know you had a brother.''

She sighed and looked terribly sad. ''Adam's been gone a long time. Yesterday you called me Beth, and it made me start thinking about him. He called me

Beth. He was the only one who ever called me anything but Elizabeth.''

''Are memories of him pleasant?''

She smiled wistfully. ''Very. Adam was my hero.''

''Then maybe I'll call you Beth all the time, too.''

''I'd like that,'' she said.

Her smile was shy, and her cheeks took on a pinker hue. When he met her he'd never have thought he'd see the day Elizabeth Boyer would look so shy—so vulnerable. No. Not Elizabeth. Beth. Today she looked like a Beth. In fact, since he picked her up for the ball, she had been Beth. He hadn't realized it till now.

Admittedly, the alliteration of Beth Boyer sounded pretty lame, but Beth Alton had an awfully nice ring. Jackson found himself fighting to keep a grin off his face. Her next words had him going from pleased as punch to angry enough to chew nails in one second flat.

''I think nearly everyone forgets Adam ever existed,'' she said. ''I was never allowed to ask about him or even say his name after he left. I was eleven years old when he left right after high school to go into the Navy. The day he left was the day he told my parents that he'd enlisted. I only saw him for a few minutes after that.''

She looked at her hands, twining and untwining them. ''The way I acted that day is one of my greatest regrets. I was furious with him for leaving me behind. I can still remember him hugging me good-bye even though I had my arms crossed and my chin buried in my chest. I wouldn't talk to him. He told me I'd understand one day why he had to leave, and I do but…''

''Maybe you should contact him?'' Jackson suggested, hating that her parents had taken away something as precious as her brother. Hating the way she refused to look at him—as if she'd done something to be ashamed of.

''I wouldn't know how to find him. Besides, if he wanted to see me, he'd have contacted me years ago.''

''Not necessarily. You were a little girl when he last saw you. You could have grown up the image of your parents. It could be that he isn't sure of his reception.''

''You think?''

Jackson nodded. ''Sure. You could probably reach him through the Navy.''

''My parents would—'' Her grin was suddenly mischievous. ''What was it you said yesterday? Have a cow. Maybe I will anyway.''

''That's the spirit.'' And he'd thought this woman would bow to her parents' obvious bad opinion of him? Once again he saw he couldn't have been more wrong about her. ''When the kids get back, we could take a ride. Maybe I could run over to my place and toss a snack together and we could eat it somewhere pretty.''

She shot him a smile he couldn't quite interpret. ''And I know just the spot.''

* * *

Elizabeth gave Glory her head and took a fence, leaving Jackson on the other side. Since he believed that if horses were supposed to fly, God would have given them wings, he rode out of his way till he came to the gate. Then he had to open it and, after closing it behind him, catch up. He shouted that she was unfair to a poor chickenhearted country boy but she just laughed and prodded her mare into a leisurely canter, secure in the knowledge that Jackson would eventually catch up after she beat him to their destination.

She rode over the hill toward the stream at the border between Laurel Glen and Boyerton, her parents' estate, and the sound of hooves thundering toward her filled her ears. Startled Elizabeth turned to see Jack as he flew by, hunkered down in his Western saddle. His laughter floated behind him the way hers probably had a few minutes earlier.

He was on the ground feigning a relaxed, lazy pose by the time she rounded the last bend. ''What took you so long?'' he asked, trying to mask his rapid breathing.

She fought a grin. He was gleefully unrepentant. ''We said race, not fly. That looked more like flying to me than taking a little fence. How can you claim to be afraid of jumping then turn around and ride at breakneck speed on unfamiliar ground?''

Jack shrugged. ''It's just the way I was raised, ma'am,'' he said, his accent purposely thick as he looked around. ''So this is the place you wanted to show me?''

''There are Lenape arrowheads all over the place. I even found an ax head once. I think they must have lived on the banks of this stream.''

Jack stooped, sifted through some stone and came up with one honed into a point. ''Incredible. I never thought there would still be a Native American site in the east. I assumed they'd have all been destroyed by development.''

Elizabeth grimaced. ''Not a good subject right now. My father owns the land on the far side of the creek. He wants to sell to developers but he has a problem because Boyerton is wedge-shaped and has very little access to the roads. Ross holds most of our property in a land lock and he won't sell access to the back section.''

''You don't seem to be angry about that.''

''I'm not. Ross has every right to keep Laurel Glen intact. Actually, I'm grateful. This was my retreat once upon a time.'' She didn't add that she had only been there with Jeff or Cole since Jason Lexington's attack made her fearful of traveling too far afield alone. It was with a measure of trust that she'd brought Jack there, and until that moment it hadn't entered her mind to be afraid. Better, she wasn't the least bit uncomfortable being there with him.

''Why doesn't your father ask Ross to buy his land, then?''

''Ross offered a couple years ago. My father can't stand Ross, so he refused. When my brother left and I refused to talk to him, Maggie told me I was cutting off my nose to spite my face. That's exactly what my father did. Since then things have gotten worse financially for both of them. My father isn't very good with finances, and with all that happened with Laurel Glen and Harry Donovan's crimes last year, I doubt Ross could afford the land right now. My father's currently talking to a developer who wants to buy up the land the carriage house sits on and demolish it to gain access to this land. My parents would be left with the house and a few acres mostly on the back side of the house, with an access road to whatever they build running within a hundred feet of their front door. Mother is having a fit.''

"And throwing rich men at you hoping for a rescue."

She sighed. "Exactly. Shall we have our snack?"

Jack pointed to a big old shade tree. She thought it was a chestnut. Next he pulled the ties off the blanket he carried on the back of his saddle and handed it to her. The smell of goldenrod was on the air, but she didn't think it smelled nearly as nice as Jack did.

As she strolled over to spread the thick Navajo blanket that felt more like a rug, Elizabeth heard the sound of leather creaking against leather as Jack pulled the saddlebags he'd packed with apples and cheese and fresh cider. She was kneeling when he dropped the bags between them and hunkered down to unpack the feast he'd put together.

"Pardon my saying this but your mother and father don't look like very happy people."

"I don't think they are. My mother only married Father for the house and the status of the Boyer name.

That's going downhill fast. He's only ever cared about what others thought of him. The adulation faded pretty quickly when his money dwindled.''

"Pretty sad way to live," he said, putting down the knife he'd been cutting the apples with.

"Very." She took a deep breath then snagged a piece of cheese and apple as he poured the cider. "Goodness, such a dreary topic on such a lovely day. So tell me about this history degree you have. Why history and not animal husbandry or some other ranching thing?"

"I had finance and—" He chuckled. "—ranching things as an undergrad. My masters is in history. It can be a little isolated at the Circle A, and continuing to take classes seemed like a good way to meet new people."

"Women, you mean," she said, feeling a little twinge of jealousy she knew she had no right to feel.

"Well, yeah." He looked uncomfortable suddenly. "But none of them ever wanted to stay in Colorado or with me. I did find a love of history, though."

So he'd been looking for love. Elizabeth definitely didn't want to think about the women he'd tried to love. "Have you been to the historic sites in Philadelphia or in the surrounding counties? We had flourishing cities and towns here when no white man had ever walked in Colorado."

"Ah. Progress." It wasn't hard to hear the sarcasm in his voice. She wondered what kept him at Laurel Glen if he longed so for home, but decided against asking. She wasn't sure she was ready for his answer.

"Not necessarily progress," she countered. "But certainly an older non-Native American culture than you'd find so far west unless you looked as far as California, anyway. And without those men and women who inhabited the original thirteen colonies, the revolution would never have happened."

She glanced at her watch and smiled while snatching another piece of juicy apple. "And we'd be having tea right now—yummy. Little dry sandwiches and hot tea." She took a sip of her cider, and the taste exploded in her mouth. "So why haven't you been to see Old City if you love history?"

"Old City? I hadn't heard of a city called old."

"Oops, sorry. Local reference. There's a section of center-city Philadelphia locals refer to as Old City. There are all sorts of historic houses and buildings in an area of several blocks. I think you'd enjoy it."

Jack shook his head. "Those expressways into the city are a little daunting to a country boy."

"Oh, knock off the cornpone routine. It might work with elitists like my parents, but you have a masters in history, for goodness' sake. I'd be glad to go in with you and show you around, though."

Jack smiled, and his brilliant blue eyes shone even in the shadow of his wide brimmed hat. "I'd like that just fine, Beth. I'm off next Saturday, if that would be good for you."

The affection in his voice when he said Beth made Elizabeth's breath catch. All she could do was nod and watch his smile broaden. He was coming to care for her and she for him. But would she ever find the courage to trust him body and soul? And even if she did, would he turn from her once he learned the dark secret she had yet to find the courage to share with him?

Where did one find courage?

Chapter Twelve

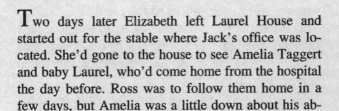

Two days later Elizabeth left Laurel House and started out for the stable where Jack's office was located. She'd gone to the house to see Amelia Taggert and baby Laurel, who'd come home from the hospital the day before. Ross was to follow them home in a few days, but Amelia was a little down about his absence, so Elizabeth had spent an extra hour there.

She had promised to have lunch with Jack that day, after she worked with Glory, which she had yet to do. Faced with a choice between working in a dusty ring with an animal who would rather have a good run or eating lunch with Jack, there was no contest.

She'd be having lunch with Jack.

Whenever she thought of him a little thrill shot through her. Which was admittedly a first for her. She was pretty sure she was coming to love him, and it looked as if her attraction for him grew exponentially. She felt more for him than she'd ever felt for any man but there were still dark shadows hovering at the edge of her life, dimming the future and its possibilities.

Over the years she'd developed a one-day-at-a-time life philosophy. While it hadn't been a cure for her problems it had kept her going. So since there seemed to be nothing she could do to chase the shadows away, she decided to accept what happiness came to her while she was with Jack in the hope that joy would keep the shadows at bay. Lunch in Jack's office might not thrill a lot of other women but to her it was a near miraculous chance to feel like a normal woman—for a little while, anyway.

In the stable she could hear the faint sound of Jack speaking over the quiet whinnies of the horses. She peeked around the corner into his office and found that he was on the phone.

His back was to her as he spoke while he gazed out the window behind his desk. "Look, Dad," he said on what sounded like a tired sigh. "I told you before, you're taking this all wrong. This is about more than that. I needed to get away, and moving into the cabin just wasn't enough. I'm thirty-two years old, and you're constantly second-guessing my every move at the ranch. Ross Taggert gives me more latitude at Laurel Glen than you ever did. If I have an idea, you assume it's no good because it's mine."

Jack's hand beat an impatient tattoo on his desk as he continued, "Well, that's how it feels from my end and I figure my emotions should count for something for a change. And Crystal's, too! Yours have been dominating our family for years.''

Feeling as if she were an intruder, Elizabeth backed away, but she knocked over a stray pitchfork in the aisle. The heavy thud drew Jack's attention. He swung around, and a look of surprise and something more settled on his face. ''Hold on a minute, will you, Dad?'' He covered the mouthpiece. ''Beth. I, uh…''

''You're talking to your father. I heard,'' she said, surprised that he was so flustered. Thinking he might be embarrassed that she'd overheard his sharp words to his father, she smiled, hoping to put him at ease. If anyone should understand having disagreements with a parent, she should. ''This is more important. I'll just catch you for lunch another day.''

''No,'' he protested. ''Hold up there. I won't be long. Lunch with you is more important than a years-old struggle with my father. We're not going to settle anything. Believe me.''

He went back to his call. ''Listen, Dad. I never said I'd be gone permanently. But I have to do this. I know you don't understand why, and right now I can't fully explain it, either. Just believe this is more about *me* than anything else. Okay?''

He listened for a long moment, his brow slightly furrowed. ''No, I don't like the sound of it, either. Get Crystal to call me. Maybe she'll talk to me.'' He paused again, listening. ''Okay? Good. I'll try, too,'' he replied and then blinked and took the phone away from his ear and shot the receiver's earpiece a quick look of disbelief before putting the phone back against his head. "I love you too, Dad," he said, sounding as confused as he looked. "Be talkin' to you soon."

He hung up the phone then, a faraway look of bewilderment still on his face.

"Is everything all right?" she asked, concerned because Jack was always so together.

"My dad said he loved me. He never says anything like that. You know it but you never hear it, you know?"

Elizabeth grimaced. "Not really," she said automatically—truthfully. She instantly regretted her candor when he looked stricken. Not wanting to let anything overshadow her chance for a few uncomplicated moments with him, she quickly changed the subject. "I heard you mention someone named Crystal. I take it that's your sister."

He nodded. "She wasn't home so I couldn't talk to her. Apparently she and her pickup had a little disagreement with a tree and another car last night. Her truck lost so she's out getting an estimate on the damage. Trouble is, it's the second freak accident she's had in a week, and Dad says she's acting a little weird. I wish I was there but—" He stared at her, and Elizabeth found her gaze captured and held by his. "But I'm not about to leave here any time soon."

Elizabeth took from his frank stare that she was the reason. "Oh," she said and her face heated, sure she'd read him correctly.

Jack grinned and sat back in his chair, gazing across the expanse of his desk at her with a satisfied look in his blue eyes. "Good. You've gotten that far, at least," he said, then he pulled a small picnic hamper from behind his desk. "I asked Ross's cook, Ruth Ann, if she knew what you'd like for lunch. She made lunch instead of just telling me what to fix. I confess I was hoping for something along those lines. My expertise doesn't get past coffee, omelettes, three-minute eggs and egg salad."

Elizabeth laughed. "Ruth Ann would say you make the egg salad when you forget to time the three-minute eggs."

He winked. "Got it in one, sweetheart," he said, Bogart style.

Her stomach flipped, and Elizabeth almost shot to her feet in an automatic flight response, but then she looked at Jack. Really looked at him. And understood. It was not fear she felt but desire.

Jackson watched Beth's eyes widen and prayed she wouldn't bolt. It was clear he'd done something that had made her suddenly aware of him as a man. He wasn't sure what. So he quickly sent a prayer winging heavenward, asking God to give her calm. Then he added one for wisdom for himself and healing for her.

He'd done a lot of praying these last few days since coming to understand the unfathomable while knowing he didn't understand at all. Someone had been so callous as to hurt her, and he couldn't grasp how anyone could injure someone as kindhearted and intrinsically good as Beth.

What really frustrated him was, now that he had a

vague idea of the problem he faced where she was concerned, he still didn't have a clue about exactly what had happened to turn her so skittish where men were concerned. Once again he wished he knew but he fought the urge to ask. While he needed desperately to know, he also knew the knowledge had to come voluntarily. Eventually she would tell him. He would earn her trust, and she would come to trust him, then she would tell him.

Jackson tore his gaze from hers and his thoughts from her problems and started pulling the food out of the basket. He wanted to enjoy this time with his Beth. Just a few minutes ago, when he'd seen her standing in the doorway, he'd thought he'd ruined everything. He'd been sure when he saw the look of distress on her face that she had overheard more than he was currently at liberty to divulge. More than he was comfortable with her learning by accident. But it was clear he'd been speaking to his father in general enough terms that the conversation had meant nothing to her. He knew he could settle back and enjoy these quiet moments.

"Ruth Ann said you like her chicken salad," he said, arranging one of the sandwiches on a plate.

Beth moaned in pleasure. "Ruth Ann's chicken salad is to die for. She toasts slivered almonds and puts them in it along with cut-up grapes." Her eyes widened even more when she looked at her plate. "Oh, and she put it on her homemade croissants! Have you had these?" She smiled widely when he shook his head. "You're in for a treat. You must be pretty special to Ruth Ann."

Jackson handed over her sandwich after putting the German potato salad and carrot sticks the cook had also sent along on the plate. Next he popped the top on a can of cola and handed it over the desk before making his own plate. "I have a feeling it was you she was treating, Beth," he said casually.

"Me?"

"How come you find that so hard to believe?"

"I've rarely been special to anyone. So, tell me about Crystal. Do you two look alike?"

Jack again felt he was withholding the truth, though the truth of his parentage wouldn't affect his relationship with her. "Not at all," he said. Remembering the pictures in his wallet, he pulled the scarred leather billfold from his back pocket, then set the picnic basket on the floor next to him. "I have pictures."

He showed her the one of Crystal she'd had taken for the paper when she was supposed to be getting engaged. She'd looked so happy. Her bright smile lit her dark eyes.

"Her hair is simply gorgeous," Elizabeth said and, thankfully, didn't comment on the lack of resemblance—but she would soon when she saw the rest.

His father's picture was next in line. Someone else he didn't look very much like. Not for the first time he wondered what it was about the human condition that they could explain away even the most startling evidence if there was something they didn't want to see. He'd forgiven his father for the years of lies, but not because he wanted to. Because he'd had to. Since then, he'd been waiting on the promise of the Lord to feel that forgiveness. When he'd heard his father say he loved him a few minutes ago, Jackson had realized he'd come to the place where he did indeed feel the forgiveness he'd granted weeks ago.

"Your father's very handsome. A lot younger than I'd expected. Is he as tall as his son?"

"Almost. When I was little I thought he'd start to notice me if I could get as tall as him." He pursed his lips and shrugged, telling himself it didn't matter. "Then I was taller and I didn't care anymore." He braced himself as she flipped to the next.

"Grandmother," he explained when she looked a little puzzled.

Though only half Cheyenne, his grandmother had been a traditional dresser. As a Christian she hadn't practiced her Cheyenne religion, but she had been very proud of her Native American ancestry. She had told them the old stories the way Europeans tell the stories of Greek and Roman mythology. And she had spoken the language to them, though not as much in later years. Consequently he'd forgotten much of what he'd learned as a youngster.

"Now I understand your sister's hair. Your grandmother is Native American." She chuckled. "I guess you all are." She tilted her head, considering him. "You don't look at all like them. But you don't take after your father, either. Sort of like me. Except I'm sure you were never an ugly duckling."

"Growing up I decided I was a conglomeration of

several generations worth of recessive genes,'' he said, not adding that in the last few months he'd come to understand that he'd been wrong. ''And I wish you'd stop calling yourself names. All children are beautiful. I don't understand your parents referring to you as an ugly duckling and thinking it was funny.''

''Tell me about your grandmother,'' she said, clearly changing the subject.

''She was Mama's mother. When Mama died she stayed to help raise us. Except she did most of the raising. She was tough. Fair. Meaner than a cornered snake if you got her riled. Wise. There was nothing that woman couldn't think her way around. She worked right up until the hour she died. Fixed dinner and scrubbed the kitchen floor then she went and sat down in her chair in front of the fire. We figured for a short nap. Crystal and I found her there when we came in from the calving shed. Dinner was still warm.''

''Oh, that's so sad. You had no warning.''

Jack shook his head. ''No. It's the way she'd have wanted it. She was doing what made her happy right up to the end—staying useful. She would have hated to be reduced to a rocking chair on the front porch. This way she never knew a sick day. She just stopped one day and went home to be with the Lord.''

''Whenever Meg talks about dying she says it the same way. Going home. Maggie, too.''

''Is that the same Maggie you mentioned that day you told me about how you got started with the women's shelter?''

She smiled and nodded. "Maggie O'Neill. She was our housekeeper. She fell and broke her hip. She's the reason I hate to see my father make a deal with that developer. If he sells the carriage house, I'll have to move into the house with them."

"That makes no sense."

"Sure it does."

"Beth, move out on your own."

"I can't. I use the money to support Maggie that I'd be spending on rent. Her hip was a severe break and she needs care. She lives in a managed-care facility that her Social Security would never cover. She was supposed to have a pension but my father made a mistake investing it in a losing venture-capital scheme."

"And you're picking up the slack for your father." It wasn't a question. He really had come to know her.

She'd taken a bite of her sandwich so she shook her head then washed down the food with her cola. "For Maggie. I do it for Maggie. She was our housekeeper from the time I was born but she took care of us like she was our nanny because she wanted to. She was more a mother to me than my mother was. Now it's my turn to care for her. It's just that it's a hundred dollars a day and—"

"That's three thousand dollars a month! How much of your salary are you shelling out?"

She shrugged as if dismissing her generosity. "Almost all of it. But I have a trust fund from my grandfather that pays my expenses."

"Except if your father sells the carriage house,

you'll have to move in with your parents. Beth, they'll drive you nuts in a week at the outside.''

Her smile was wry, and she sighed. "I know. But I'm a lot tougher than I look."

She'd have to be, because right then she looked like a marshmallow. Soft and sweet. He wanted desperately to circle the desk and kiss her but he knew that wasn't a good idea.

Jackson walked her to her car half an hour later, still wishing for that kiss but determined to fight his need. He didn't want her bolting again.

"Thank Ruth Ann for me for lunch," she said, turning to him when she reached her car.

"Sure." He was disappointed their short interlude was over. He didn't want to wait till their Saturday sight-seeing excursion to see her again. "I mentioned dinner out the other day. Would you like to check out that little Thai place that just opened?"

"I'd like that," she said, smiling.

Jackson felt a little light-headed as relief spread through him. He sucked in a deep breath and, as his oxygen-starved lungs filled with air, he realized he'd been holding his breath. But he didn't think that was the reason for his light-headedness. He was sure it had more to do to with the scent that had filled his head the minute she'd walked into his office. Much more to do with those clear, green-as-emerald eyes of hers. And a whole lot more to do with hair that looked and felt like corn silk and skin that reminded him of the richest cream.

"Tomorrow night?" he asked, surprised at how husky his voice sounded.

"As long as it isn't till seven. I have to be at work till about six."

"Seven's perfect."

Chapter Thirteen

Elizabeth had one hand on the car door while the other clutched the purse that hung on her shoulder. Just a few minutes ago Jack had glanced at the clock over his door and blinked in astonishment. She, too, had done a double take when she'd seen how late it was—how quickly their lunchtime together had flown by.

When he'd stood to walk her to her car, Elizabeth had been inordinately touched by the gallant gesture and the tenderness in his eyes. Looking at him with the sky behind him bright with promise and the air sweet and just a little sultry, she felt another surprising emotion. Before she could think about it or what it meant, she reached out and, using his shoulders for balance, stood on tiptoe to kiss his cheek.

"Thanks for lunch," she said, her voice breathless all of a sudden. Then she quickly turned and climbed into her car before Jack had a chance to comment. Of course, there was every chance he wouldn't have said a thing since he'd looked as if she'd hit him over the head instead of pecking him on the cheek.

She wondered if he were still standing there. As she approached the beginning of the driveway she looked back to wave and gave into a little bubble of laughter. Her heart started beating in time to one of Mr. Sousa's marches—the triumphant one playing in her head. Jack still stood in the same spot, still as a statue, with his fingertips covering his cheek.

Maybe it was her euphoria that caused her to be careless. After she'd been driving for a good five minutes, Elizabeth realized that for the first time in weeks she'd forgotten to check that she wasn't being followed on her way to the New Life Inn.

She casually glanced in the rearview mirror and nearly screamed. A car that looked very much like Brian Hobart's was behind her.

Telling herself she was being a hysterical fool, Elizabeth nonetheless turned at the next road just to be safe. Like the section of Indian Creek Road Laurel Glen sat on, there was nothing on Coventry Drive but a few scattered homes set far back from the road. Chances were the car behind her wouldn't follow. Seconds after she made her turn, the silver, high-end luxury car followed her onto Coventry.

Instinct made her speed up, and she quickly realized the car matched her speed, though it still hung back, not crowding her or threatening her. Knowing she couldn't chance going to the shelter in case she wasn't being an utter fool, Elizabeth made another right then a left, desperately wanting to get to Jack. He wouldn't laugh at her. He would hold her. He would tell her she'd been smart not to take a chance.

Elizabeth soon realized she'd made two errors. The second road she'd turned on, Hunt Club Lane, led her toward Laurel Glen but on a parallel road. The turn apparently alerted whoever was behind her to the fact that she knew he was following her, since her course made no sense. She glanced back just in time to see Brian Hobart's furious expression as he rammed her from behind. Elizabeth floored her accelerator before her mind grasped what had happened, thus minimizing some of the impact.

Shooting forward and away from immediate danger, she tried to think rationally. Though her sporty little car couldn't take much of that kind of punishment from a much bigger car, it could outmaneuver Hobart's on the twisting back roads. She grabbed her cell phone and she hit her redial button, knowing it was Jack's number. He'd know what to do. She knew he would.

Just as she put the little phone on its hands-free mode, Jack answered.

"Jack," she cried, not surprised to hear her voice quake. "Hobart's behind me. He rammed me but I got away. What do I do? I just turned onto Stoney Hollow off of Hunt Club. He's gaining on me on the straight section I'm on right now."

"I'll get the police moving in your direction. If you see anybody in a field or on a mower, attract their attention even if you have to drive through a fence.

He's a coward. He won't do anything with a witness there. Just don't try for a house. Chances are you'd pick someplace where no one's home, and those places are too secluded. I'm coming, sweetheart.''

She could tell he was running as he spoke. She heard him shout instructions to someone about calling the police and about her location. Then his engine roared to life.

"I'm in my truck, Beth. Hang in there. Are you coming toward Laurel Glen?" he asked, his voice utterly calm.

"I think that's what tipped him off."

"That's okay. It gets you closer to me. I'll be coming at you from this end of Stoney Hollow."

Her mind on the road ahead, Elizabeth wasn't ready when Hobart caught up and rammed her as she took a tight curve. Elizabeth screamed as the little car lost purchase on the dusty road and went into a spin. She wound up on the shoulder, the front grillwork of the silver monster just behind her door. Hobart had pinned her car against a high dirt wall at the side of the road. She floored the accelerator but her tires spun ineffectively, the back end of the car off the surface enough to make escape impossible.

Once the noise of the collision ceased, she heard Jack on the speaker frantically calling to her. "Jack. Hurry. He rammed me again and I spun out. He has my car pinned against a dirt embankment."

"Lock your doors!"

"They are." She sobbed then screamed when Hobart appeared at her side. He reached for her door handle and furiously shook her car trying to force it open. All the while he shouted insults and obscenities, ordering her to open her door. Then he pivoted and ran.

''Beth!'' she heard Jack shout. ''He can't get in. I have to be almost there.''

''He left. Maybe he hears you coming,'' she cried, but her relief was short-lived.

A shadow fell next to her, something flashed by her eye and before she could process what it was, a tremendous crash above her head sent the roof smashing into her skull. Stunned for a moment, she heard Jack call her name and beg her to answer him. Before she could, her windshield shattered.

''Get to the other side of the car, Beth. And cover your face!''

Elizabeth obeyed Jack's command instinctively. And would be ever thankful that she did. Just as she pulled her legs over the console and turned away from the window the driver's side window shattered in hundreds of dangerous shards and exploded all over the interior.

Then rough hands dragged her across the glass-encrusted driver's seat. She tried to hold onto the wheel in spite of the fact that glass was embedded in her arms, but Hobart was as strong as an enraged bull. He grasped her hair and yanked. She screamed and heard Jack bellow her name from the phone's speaker. His fear for her was a living thing in his voice. And she knew she'd dragged Jack into her worst nightmare.

Hobart spun her to face him and shoved her against his car. He still held her hair. "Where is she?" he demanded.

"Please. Let go of me. She isn't at the shelter anymore. So following me won't do you any good."

"Tell me where she is or you'll be sorry."

"I'm telling the truth. She's gone," she sobbed.

Elizabeth didn't see it coming. One second she was terrified and the next her mind was numb but not enough that she didn't feel her head throb or hear her ears ringing from a blow on the head.

He called her a vile name and shook her by her hair, his face a blur through her tears. "There's no way you don't know where she is," he screamed in her face.

He was so close she could feel the angry heat of his body. It was too much like the last time, and she felt her mind blink for a second, but she fought the urge to let the encroaching darkness completely engulf her.

"You'd better let me go," she told him in an unsteady voice. "I called for help on my cell phone. He'll be here any second."

"Like anyone's going to get to you this fast," he said, sneering.

He once again demanded Melissa Hobart's address and pummeled her head with his fist.

It's just like before. He's going to kill me. Dear God, help me! she prayed, desperate.

Then a roar filled her ears, and she could feel her mind dim and darken. But all at once the pitch of the roar changed, and she was pulled momentarily from the encroaching blackness. It was the roar of a powerful engine coming around the curve ahead. And it was followed by the screech of tires and brakes.

Jack.

Jackson threw his door open before his truck came to a complete stop. He slammed the transmission into neutral and stomped on the emergency brake. He could hear the police sirens from a distance, but his only concern was Beth. Hobart looked toward him, then tossed her into the road like a discarded rag doll.

She fell limply and lay still. Unmoving. And Jackson's thundering heart nearly stopped. He wanted to hold her in his arms and protect her. Make sure she was all right.

Screaming obscenities at him, Hobart turned to his car, and Jackson ran toward him. If Hobart backed up to make a run for it, Beth would be on the road in his path. Then the miserable coward stopped with one foot in the car and glanced toward the sound of sirens approaching.

Jackson saw the truth dawn on him. The pickup blocked the road ahead, and the cops were coming from behind. He couldn't get out of this.

Hobart's cold eyes cut to Beth's still form. He charged toward her, clearly intending to use her as a hostage. Without a moment's thought, Jackson launched himself at the other man and took him down inches short of Beth's prone body.

Hobart might be good at beating on defenseless

women, but he had probably never done a moment's physical work in his life. Beth's attacker got in one lucky shot, but Jackson had him eating dirt in ten seconds flat. Considering the blue language Hobart was spouting, Jackson thought that was poetic justice.

The police cars rolled in. The sirens cut out, but the lights stayed on. The first cop to get to them took over with Hobart, which was fine with Jackson. He was too worried about Beth to care about revenge, but he wouldn't trust himself if Beth turned out to be seriously hurt.

He looked across the few feet that separated them and said a quick prayer that she was all right, though he'd prayed ceaselessly during those tense minutes as he'd driven like a madman trying to get to her, hearing her screams and calls for help. Each sound of distress had torn at his soul, and he knew that only the grace of God had kept him together.

"Who's who?" the first cop asked as Jackson scrambled to his feet.

"I'm Jack Alton," Jackson said and turned toward Beth. "Take care of him, will you? I want to see to Beth."

A second cop put his hand on Jackson's shoulder, blocking his way. "Can I see your driver's license?" he asked as the first cop strong-armed Hobart to his feet and another cop moved toward Beth.

Jackson understood their caution, but one thing he didn't want was Beth coming to and finding herself being handled by a stranger. "Don't touch her." He all but snarled the words and made a grab for his back pocket and his wallet.

"Let go of me," Hobart demanded. "He attacked me, officer, and, ah…hit that poor woman with his truck. I was trying—"

"Shut up, Hobart," Jackson growled, wanting more than ever to finish what he'd started.

"Go check your lady friend," cop two said before Jackson had his wallet out of his pocket. "He just confirmed your identity. We knew someone in a teal pickup from Laurel Glen was trying to get to her. We just didn't know what you look like."

Jackson nodded and rushed to Beth. She hadn't moved since Hobart tossed her aside, and his stomach gave a sick turn when he thought what that might mean.

She lay on her side, her hair covering her face. "Beth," he whispered next to her ear. *Please let her be all right,* he prayed and braced himself as he swept her hair aside. Surprisingly there was no obvious damage to her face.

So why was she unconscious?

"Sweetheart, can you hear me? It's Jack."

Her lashes flickered, and she opened her eyes. "Jack?" she asked as if confused, then she gasped and terror flooded her pale features. She'd remembered.

"It's okay," he rushed to assure her.

"You okay, miss?" the cop behind her asked.

Beth yelped and grabbed onto Jackson, scrambling

away from the voice behind her. Then she moaned and grabbed her head.

"It's okay. This is Officer—"

"Doyle," the cop said. "I think we should call an ambulance."

"No. I just want to go home," Beth told him. She looked determined.

"You need to be checked at the hospital. You were really out," Jackson explained. To the cop he said, "Suppose I take her to the ER then home if they release her? Someone could come and take our statements later."

"Sure. One of the detectives will be in touch. If you'll just give me—"

"No. You have to promise," Beth said out of the blue, grabbing his shirt. "Nobody can know. You promised not to tell. Nothing happened."

"Hobart hit you. I saw him hit you," Jackson protested.

She narrowed her eyes, her head clearly causing her a lot of pain. "Hobart? Cole, who is Hobart?"

Jackson felt as if she'd stabbed him, but then he understood the utter confusion in her gaze. It was as if she didn't know where she was. Or when. He looked at the cop. "Could you get us to the hospital?"

The cop jumped up. "Jerry, you're transporting," Jackson heard him say. "It looks like she's got a head injury."

Jackson scooped Beth into his arms and laid her on the back seat of the car, then climbed in to cradle her in his arms. She didn't seem to mind his nearness, but then again, she seemed to think he was Cole.

Beth looked at him, her green eyes large in her pale face. He could see she was in pain, and her pupils weren't reacting to the light as they went in and out of the shade. He knew the next ten minutes would be the longest of his life.

"Why won't you take me home?" she asked.

"Honey, I think you have a concussion. Try to relax. Okay?"

She nodded then winced. "I'm confused. Aren't I?" Beth asked and stared at him. He could see her trying to work something out in her befuddled mind. "You have blue eyes." Then she reached up and touched his cheekbone, a look of confused wonder on her beautiful tearstained face. "You're Jack." Her voice broke, and he knew she was remembering Hobart's attack. "You came. He smashed into me. Then he smashed the roof and the windshield. The window in the door, too." She frowned as if trying to piece together another complicated thought. "He wrecked my car. Didn't he?" She sounded like she was going to cry.

"It looked pretty smashed up, honey, but that's what insurance is for."

She scowled, and it made her look so cute and fuzzy-headed that he wanted to hug her. She's had enough trauma today, he thought sardonically.

"I really liked that car," she muttered then utterly floored him when she laid her head on his chest.

Feeling her trust seep into his heart, Jackson had

to blink back the tears that sprung to his eyes. "It was a tin can on wheels," he told her, his voice hoarse and nearly breaking. "We'll find you a good sturdy one."

But the first thing he was going to do was teach her how to defend herself the way he had Crystal. Nobody would ever overpower her so quickly again. Crystal could have cleaned Hobart's clock but good.

The cop had radioed ahead to the ER, and there was a stretcher waiting for Beth when they arrived. Jackson hated giving her over to the care of strangers, but he had little choice. She was no longer in danger from anything but her injuries.

And maybe something in her past that haunted her.

While she'd been confused about time and place for those few interminable minutes on the road and in the car, he was very much afraid she'd given him a glimpse of what had caused her to pull away from his embraces in anger and fear. It looked as if her fight-or-flight reflex was caused by a fear he wasn't sure how to fight. Jackson pursed his lips and deliberately pushed out of his mind the appalling possibility that she feared physical and not emotional danger.

Resolutely, needing to find a little peace and calm, Jackson headed for the chapel, trying to empty his mind of all but prayers of thanksgiving for her safety. Because if he thought about what her confused pleas for secrecy had meant, he'd lose what was left of his composure.

And there wasn't much left to lose.

He was angrier than he'd ever been in his life, especially since lifting her out of the car. He hadn't seen the blood until then—the cuts marring the creamy soft skin of her arms. Her blood stained his shirt and jeans and reminded him every time he glanced at himself of her cries of terror and pain while she'd been out of his reach. Just the thought of Hobart with his hand on Beth—hurting Beth—had been enough without finding her injured. And knowing something similar may have happened to her before was a little more than he could handle on his own.

The last time he felt the urge to pummel someone with his fists in vengeance had been in junior high when he'd come upon Joey King yanking on Crystal's pigtails and tormenting her. The schoolyard bully also had been calling his little sister filthy, derogatory names because of her Native American heritage. Jackson had gone after the older boy and all but taken him apart before teachers intervened.

His father would say he'd come a long way from that furious preteen who'd refused to apologize to Joey King. And he had. He'd restrained himself today against the urge to do more than subdue Brian Hobart, but he still couldn't get to a place where it *felt* wrong to use his fists to avenge a loved one against a bully.

As he settled into one of the dark wood pews of the little chapel, he decided restraint must be a lot like forgiveness. It was something you did even if you didn't feel like it.

Chapter Fourteen

Elizabeth forced her grainy eyes open and found herself in a darkened room. There was ambient light coming from around a miniblind that had been closed so she knew it wasn't night. Her head hurt less than before, and her mind felt clear. She purposely retraced her steps through the day, looking for holes in her memory.

She'd slept late, not getting up till around ten. After tea and toast for breakfast she'd picked some flowers for her mantel, then had gone to see Amelia Taggert and baby Laurel. She'd stayed too long and had opted to forgo riding Glory to spend her remaining time having lunch with Jack.

She smiled, thinking of her time with him. Who would ever think exchanging stories and pictures of the people in your life could be so much fun? Or that you could learn so much about a person with the use of a few props?

Then she'd kissed him good-bye and had driven straight into a nightmare. She remembered thinking she'd dragged Jack into it by her desperate phone call for help.

The whole thing came back to her in a rush. Being rammed from behind that first time. Then again. The spin. The way Brian Hobart had steered into the side of her car and pinned it against the embankment. Seeing a flash of the tire iron in his hand just before he sent the roof of her special little car crashing down on her head. Then the windshield imploding and the sound and sting of the glass of her driver's side window exploding inward against her back and arms. Being dragged out of the car, and the sick certainty that leveling blows to the head was a technique Hobart had perfected on Melissa Hobart so no one would see what he'd done. She and Melissa were both lucky to be alive.

She must have made a sound of distress because a chair scraped nearby and Jack's concerned face came into view.

That's when she remembered he'd been there when she woke on the side of the road, confused and disoriented. She remembered his tender care of her. And the pain that had rocketed across his features when she'd called him Cole.

What am I going to say to you, Jack? How can I explain?

Then he had called her Beth. Guilt, worry and fear melted away in a millisecond. This was Jack.

"It's okay. You're safe," he had told her.

Something about him saying that bothers me. Why?

"Beth, there's a detective here to see you. Are you up to telling them what happened?"

Why is he treating me like spun glass?

"They're pretty sure they can keep a judge from setting bail for Hobart again. So if you don't want to see them, it's okay. But they want to prove to the judge that this is related to the charges Melissa Hobart filed against him. They say that would cinch it. I'd feel better if I were sure they could keep him in jail till his trial. I'm sure you would, too."

Elizabeth frowned. "Of course, I'll talk to them. Why would you think I wouldn't?"

He shrugged and turned toward the door. As his eyes slid away, the look she saw there opened yet another memory. When she'd come to on the road, he'd said something to the officer about her making a statement later. And she'd thought he was Cole and was about to break his word about keeping her secret. And that memory answered both her spoken and unspoken questions.

He knew. Somehow he knew.

She looked at Jack, at the pain on his face, and knew she had hurt him. Would continue to hurt him. Until she could face the past and explain it to him. But she couldn't face the thought of revealing the painful truth of her past in a place so impersonal. "I want to go home after this, Jack."

He nodded. "I'll see if I can move things along."

Elizabeth roused from an uneasy doze, a light metallic click invading her consciousness. She turned her head and saw Jack carefully close his driver's side door and stride away from the truck to open the front door of her carriage house. Within seconds he returned and quietly opened the door at her side.

"Glad you could join me," he quipped when he saw she was awake. His grin clearly wasn't as lighthearted as he pretended, however. "Planning to stay around long?" he went on. "Or are you going to make a habit of falling asleep in the middle of a sentence?"

"I feel much more rested. I think I can stay awake now."

"Too little, too late. You have no idea how disturbing it is to be right in the midst of a shortcut and have your guide start snoring in your ear."

She smiled at his attempt to tease her and appear relaxed. Did he really think she was fooled? While she'd given her statement to the state police detective, Jack had hovered next to her like a mother hen protecting its chicks. When the detective asked if Brian Hobart had touched her in a sexual way, the comparison had notched up closer to that of an angry mama grizzly. And he'd been a bundle of nerves since the doctor gave him the list of instructions for her care, so she wasn't fooled a bit by his attempt at levity.

"Jack, I'm fine," she told him, hating the tight look in his eyes, which he was trying to hide. And it was that much worse because it was two parts worry and two parts hurt. "I truly do feel much better," she went on, lying for a good cause. ''The headache isn't so bad now.''

''Good. It's one of the warning signs I promised to watch for. If it gets worse, you have to tell me.'' He let out a deep breath and scooped her up into his strong arms.

''Jack!'' she shrieked.

''Humor me. They warned me you could get dizzy,'' he said and vaulted up the steps.

Though he'd surprised her, Elizabeth realized she'd instinctively looped her arms around his neck. Their lips were a fraction of an inch apart when he looked at her once he reached the front door. The expression on his face was so tender her breath caught. She thought he might kiss her.

''I—I could have walked, Jack.''

''No need. I've got you.''

Twenty minutes later, he walked into her cozy parlor with a tray in his hands.

''You don't have to wait on me.''

He affected the worst imitation of dejection she'd ever seen. ''I don't prepare my special cinnamon and sugar toast for just anyone, you know. And I'm told by connoisseurs worldwide my tea is always brewed to perfection. I am so underappreciated around here. It's a crying shame.'' He set the tray down.

''What's a crying shame is your dubious acting ability.''

''That means you can always trust me. You'll always know exactly what I'm thinking by my expression.''

Yes, she would. She couldn't help but remember the look on his face when she'd called him Cole.

Will that day haunt me forever? And now Jack.

She lay there looking at his beloved face. I can't let you go, she thought. But I can't even try to keep you in my life if I can't get past Jason Lexington— if I can't at least share it with you so you understand.

"You want to talk about it?" he asked as if reading her mind.

"No. I want to see you smile but I guess that's asking a bit much."

He closed his eyes and said on a sigh, "Oh, yeah."

"I'm sorry I didn't know you at first when I woke up on the road."

He shook his head and sat on the ottoman near the sofa. He picked up her hand, holding it gently and stroking it with his fingertips. "Not a problem. You have a concussion. Your vision was probably fuzzy."

"No. That would be an easy out, but it would be a lie. I think I've been lying to myself for long enough. I thought you were Cole. I thought he'd come to save me."

"Oh. I see," he said stiffly. The hand stroking hers had gone still.

She carefully shook her head and forced out the words he deserved. The words she had to say if she was ever going to move past that day. If she was ever going to take back her life. Not just parts, but all of it.

"No, you don't. I thought he'd come to save me—

the way he did once before." She emphasized the words.

A look of dread entered his blue eyes. He looked like he was ready to bolt. "Before?" he asked, holding his place.

"You don't have to listen if you don't want to but I thought you deserved to know. I thought maybe if I said it out loud, I'd finally start to deal with what happened."

"Then I'm here to listen," he said, encouraging her with his expression, "but would you let me do something first, Beth? Would you let me pray for you?"

She smiled. She'd never really believed a man like this existed in this I-and-me and sex-sells-everything world they lived in today. "I'm beginning to think I'd be a fool to say no to an offer like that."

He nodded and closed his eyes. She closed hers, too. He was the expert, after all.

"Father, I praise You and I thank You for Beth. She hasn't had the best of days, Lord, but You ultimately protected her from evil, and I thank You for that, too. We know that on this earth sometimes evil triumphs, but we also know it's only for a season. I ask You to release Beth from whatever hold the past has on her. I beg You to strengthen her and help her as she talks about whatever puts such pain in her pretty eyes. Amen."

"I don't deserve you," she whispered.

He squeezed her hand gently. "Suppose you tell me what happened to blind you to how special you are."

Elizabeth wondered if he'd still feel that way after she explained. She wondered if she could even say the words that would destroy his high opinion of her. She bit her lip and looked at her hands as he let go of them.

She nearly snatched his hand back, feeling suddenly bereft of his touch, but she forced herself to begin her tale. Alone. The way she'd been back then.

"Remember I told you I was an ugly duckling when I was younger? I know you were incensed that I'd ever heard that from my mother, but my family weren't the only ones who felt that way. Do you remember the story of the ugly duckling?"

He shrugged. "I got stories of coyote and rabbit at home, but I have a vague memory of it."

"Well, the story is that everyone at the pond made fun of the ugly duckling because he was different. Even his siblings and eventually his mother. In school the other kids made fun of me. One day when I was fourteen, just after my braces came off, they went from calling me Frizzy Lizzie and tinsel teeth to an even nastier, more personal kind of teasing. I couldn't take it anymore, so I decided to leave the school before the end of the day."

Elizabeth heard her voice start to lose strength. She nearly gave in to the temptation to stop, but Jack's thumb started stroking the back of her hand. She hadn't realized he'd reached out to her again.

"It's okay, Beth," he said, his voice low and soothing. "Just take your time. We all have bad memories to contend with."

"Not like this. And the worst part is that it was all my fault. If I'd only gone back to class." She sighed. "But I didn't. I'd gotten a short distance from the main building when I heard someone call my name. It was Jason Lexington. He was a senior, and so popular. He said he'd heard what they'd all been saying to me and he was sorry. He said they were jealous because he could tell I was going to be pretty some day. He said he liked my smile. He wanted to walk home with me. I remember thinking how handsome he was and how nice he was to lie so prettily just to make me feel better.

"That was my second mistake. I was flattered and I went off with him. I didn't even notice that we weren't walking toward home at first. He told me all about the car his father bought him for his birthday and about the championship game earlier in the year when he ran for the winning touchdown. When I noticed our direction, he said it was a shortcut through the woods."

Elizabeth knew she was crying because Jack kept trying to wipe her tears with his free hand, but they kept falling and she forced herself to keep talking. She'd never told it all. Cole had reported what he'd interrupted when he got her home. And her mother had put her in the shower, telling her that if she just didn't think about it, it would be as if it had never happened. But it hadn't worked out that way. It had haunted her sleep for years—her waking hours, too. Maybe in the telling some healing would start at last.

"After about fifteen minutes," she said, "I started

getting nervous and I tried to go back the way we came but he stepped in front of me and said he wanted to kiss me. That he'd been thinking about it since the first time he noticed me. I let him but then he wouldn't stop.'' She sobbed and found herself held against Jack's chest.

"I tried to run but he was so much bigger. I scratched him and he hit me and then he had a knife in his hand. He pushed me down. He held me down. He told me he'd kill me if I screamed. I thought he'd kill me anyway. I knew who he was, after all. So I screamed anyway. He put his hand on my throat and pressed till I began losing consciousness. Then he came down at my face with the knife but instead of stabbing me, he buried the knife in the ground next to my face. I stopped screaming then and just stared at the knife while he raped me.''

"Beth, you don't have to tell me anymore,'' Jack broke in.

"Yes, I do have to tell you. Please, I have to finally tell someone. I know this will change everything so I don't know why it has to be you but it does.''

"Then finish it.'' he ordered, sounding a little harsh.

She'd expected his anger but still it surprised her in a way. She gathered enough courage to look at him. He had tears on his face, which made no sense. He was supposed to be angry. Think she was damaged and soiled. Not feel her pain. That was all wrong.

Confused, she took a deep breath and did as he ordered. "Cole came before it was over. He pulled him off me and they fought. Jason finally broke away and ran. Cole put me in his own jacket and took care of me. He took me home, but he didn't really understand all of it. He didn't see the knife. Or that it was my fault for trusting Jason. Or about my parents. He told me no one could change who I was inside but he was wrong.

"My mother knew what Jason had done changed me. She told me she'd fix it so no one could see. So no one could tell. They made Cole promise not to tell anyone. They said no one would believe me or him because Jason's family was so rich and powerful. My father said we'd all be destroyed if I pressed charges, Cole's father as well as my parents."

"I'm sure they were trying to protect you," he whispered, but she could tell he didn't believe it, either.

"You know they're ashamed of me. I was stupid and vain to listen to Jason Lexington's lies. It's what they think. I know that's what you're thinking. It has to be."

Because if it isn't, if this doesn't push you away, I don't think I can give you up. And this terror inside me may destroy us both.

Chapter Fifteen

Jackson held her away from him and tried to get a handle on his anger at her parents. What had they done to their child? Were they so selfish that her seemingly distorted interpretation was on the mark?

"I'm not thinking anything like that. And I can't imagine they would, either. That's a complete load of garbage, Beth."

Her eyes lit with anger. "No, it isn't. Don't try to lie to me. I overheard my parents that night. They took a hundred thousand dollars for not pressing charges. My father said it was for damages but not those done to me. They've never even mentioned the money to me. It was for damage to *them!* He told my mother Jason would get away with it anyway if I pressed charges and then everyone would know about what I'd done. They wouldn't be able to hold their heads up in public. He blamed me for putting them in such a bad position. They *were* ashamed of me."

She lifted her head and held it at a defiant tilt. "So I left, just the way the duckling ran away from the pond. He found the wild geese who were kind of like outlaws but they were happy to have him with them. I found Cole. I wanted to embarrass them so badly they wouldn't have been able go out of their house to spend their blood money or look their friends in the eye."

"Oh, honey," he sighed, afraid for the child she'd been. Jackson had heard stories of Cole's destructive period after the death of his mother. He would have been exactly what she needed that night. A strange combination of safety and danger. "What happened?"

"Ross and Cole had argued because he was all bruised up and wouldn't tell how it happened. He'd stormed off, furious that his father had assumed he'd been in trouble. Especially when he'd gotten hurt helping someone. Especially when he was keeping silent to keep Laurel Glen safe from Jason's family, even though he thought it was wrong.

"Cole came upon a police car running on the side of the road, got in and simply drove it away. He was my outlaw that night—my wild goose. And just like with the duckling and the wild geese, the hunt was on. Only it was the police not the hunters after us. I started to get scared when we could hear their sirens getting close. That's when Cole talked me into bailing out of the car and running home."

Jackson's estimation of his cousin rose even higher. He'd saved Beth not only from certain death at a rapist's hands but also from the folly of her anger at her parents. And to this day he was still taking flack for that night. Yet he'd never given away her secret.

"That's why you and Cole are so close. Right?"

"We are now. I never saw him again until he came back to Laurel Glen about a year and a half ago. I never forgot him, but I didn't try to contact him in all the years he was away, either."

"Why?" he asked, needing to understand this odd connection between his cousin and the woman Jackson had come to love. Not because he was in the least jealous anymore but because each piece he was able to fit together of the puzzle Beth was brought him that much closer to her.

"Why didn't I try to contact him? Because I was a coward and because my memory of him was so connected to that day. I thought seeing him again, even writing to him, would force me to think about that day."

"But you said you went to that Valentine's dance with Jeff knowing Cole would be there."

She nodded sadly. "I couldn't have lived with myself if I'd been that much of a coward. He needed help, and it was my turn to save him."

"Like you help the women at the center. And like you went to the Graystone Ball in case Cole and CJ needed protection from the Lexington women."

"Cole is a target because of me."

"You aren't a coward, Beth." Praying for restraint, he continued. "I assume Mrs. Lexington was related to Jason."

"She's his mother. Alexandra is his half sister."

Then Jack asked the question that had been burning in his chest. He truly didn't know what he'd do if the answer was yes. "Does he still live around here?"

She shook her head. "Three teenagers left Village Green within the next week all those years ago. Jason was first—headed for a European boarding school. Next Cole left for a military school. It was part of a deal Ross made with the DA. Then my mother took me to a spa in Nevada. That's where they hid me behind a pretty, fake facade. I felt so dirty inside, but they just covered it over. I always have to be so careful not to let anyone see what he did to me."

"There's no facade now, Beth." Jackson fingered her tangled hair. "Your hair's all rumpled." Next he feathered his fingertips against her face and down her neck. "Your makeup wore off hours ago." Then he skimmed his knuckles across her collarbone to her cotton-clad shoulder and fingered the wrinkled material of the hospital gown she'd had to wear home because the light sweater she'd been wearing was filled with tiny glass shards. "And I hear the fashion police are out to confiscate every one of these in the whole country. But to me you look as sweet and enchanting and *pure* as ever."

A great silent tear rolled from one of her eyes as she closed them. She said nothing when he fell silent and let his gaze drink in her loveliness.

"Where is Lexington now? Still in Europe?" he asked, a little restless after touching her but afraid to move from her side lest she misinterpret his actions with her distorted sense of the world around her. Everything he said and did from now on had to be carefully weighed. He would die before letting her assume he saw her as soiled or sullied by Lexington's violence.

"Jason's dead," she said, her voice hoarse with unshed tears and more than likely from her plaintive screams for help earlier in the day, too. "He was killed in an auto accident the following year," she went on. "Mitzy Lexington blames me and she blames Cole."

"Well, she's wrong. And you're wrong about who was at fault," he said. "Didn't any of the rape counselors you saw tell you it was all Lexington's doing? It was no more your fault than today was." He saw the guilt shadow her eyes. "Tell me you don't think today was your fault."

"If I'd checked behind me when I left Laurel Glen he—"

"Stop," he ordered softly. "You've never seen a counselor about any of this, have you?"

She ducked her head. "No."

He took her chin and raised her tear-washed eyes level with his. "I can't imagine why not, but we're going to fix that," he promised.

"You should go home to the Circle A. Your father misses you. So must your sister."

"*You* aren't at the Circle A."

Her eyes widened at what his matter-of-fact statement revealed, but she shook her head as if banishing the thought. "Exactly. You should forget about me and my…problems. They're never going to go away.''

''I don't want to go home.'' Not without you, he added silently, knowing he'd given her enough to think about where they were concerned without increasing the pressure. ''And no, they won't just go away. But your parents were wrong. You have to deal with this, not pretend it didn't happen. It did. You were hurt. Violated. And you are no more responsible for what happened to you than any of the women at the shelter are for what their husbands did to them. It's all violence. Just different weapons.''

''But—''

''But nothing. And another thing. You are never going to be that helpless again. As soon as you get the go-ahead, I'm teaching you how to defend yourself.''

She let out a giggle he knew was based more on nerves and near hysteria than levity. ''You're going to teach *me* how to box?''

He tapped her nose with his fingertip. ''I'm going to teach you self-defense. When I'm done, you'll be able to knock men like Hobart six ways from Sunday.''

She put her hand over her heart. ''But what about here? I'm no good for you this way. I'm no good for anyone. I don't know how to fix what he broke inside me.''

''That's where counseling and God come in. Isn't this why you started going to church? This is what you were looking to find peace from. This time, honey, you went looking in the right place.''

"I hope so,'' she said, her green eyes wide and imploring.

"I know so. I also know it's time you tried to rest.''

She looked suddenly stricken. "I guess you'll be going then.''

"Going? As in leaving you here alone? Not hardly,'' he said à la John Wayne. "I fully intend to stay with you tonight. At least tonight. Until I'm sure Hobart isn't granted bail.''

He could see uncertainty flood her gaze. She still had so far to go. His chest ached because of what that meant. Because until her eyes were no longer shadowed with fear, shame or guilt, there was no guarantee of a future for them.

"Beth. You're safe with me. You know that, don't you?''

She nodded.

"Good,'' he said and picked up an afghan to cover her. "Now we're getting somewhere. Suppose you hunker down, get comfy and tell me which bay downstairs I should I put my truck in. I don't want your parents seeing my truck here all night.''

"Are you really sure you want to stay?''

"Yes. I wouldn't get a wink of sleep worrying about you here all alone tonight. And I promised the doc I'd watch you. I also just promised you I'd be here till we're sure Hobart's bound over for trial. I'll do both happily. But that doesn't mean I want your parents getting the idea anything untoward is happening between us. I refuse to play fast and loose with your reputation.''

A blush rose on Beth's face, and she did as ordered. She told him where to store his truck, then fell asleep quickly even though she'd dozed most of the way home. He'd been told she probably would, but he was as nervous about her health as he was her mental state.

Which only stood to reason, with a list of possible symptoms and warning signs running through his head. He was supposed to watch for worsening headache, confusion and increasing sleepiness. Those were danger signs, and he was to call the doctor immediately. But dizziness, poor concentration, forgetfulness or depression, among other symptoms, were normal signs of post-concussion syndrome.

As he watched her sleep, Jackson was nearly overcome with worry and fear. How was he supposed to tell the difference between confusion and forgetfulness? Too much sleep and not enough? The headache she had or if she was keeping increased pain to herself? She bravely might not mention if it grew worse.

While Beth slept, Jackson called Pastor Jim Dillon at the Tabernacle, seeking advice about someone to help Beth face her nightmarish past. He learned that Dillon's wife, Holly, had taken classes in counseling women to help him with the female members of his congregation on personal matters they were reluctant to bring to him. Jackson now had someone he was sure would lead Beth in the right direction in her quest for healing. All he had to do was convince her to talk with Holly Dillon.

The ring of the telephone woke Elizabeth around ten. She heard the murmur of Jack's voice as he spoke in hushed tones to someone on the other end of the line. The parlor was in darkness but for a ribbon of light escaping the kitchen door. It lent only a soft glow to the room but it was enough so that she wasn't disoriented. Her head felt better, and what little dizziness she'd felt seemed to have abated along with her headache.

Still, she felt odd. Not physically but emotionally. Almost hollow. Numb. As if the events of the day had left her drained not only of strength but also anguish and worry. She thought perhaps her emotions had been stripped from her and all ability to feel was gone, but then Jack pushed open the door. Seeing his strong, handsome profile silhouetted against the light changed her mind instantly.

She loved him.

And she felt that emotion to the depths of her soul.

She could admit that now, but only to herself. Because she couldn't tell him. Not when she wasn't sure she'd ever be able to express that love physically. She couldn't risk hurting him again. It hurt her to remember the pain in his gaze when she'd pushed him away in the garden the night of the Graystone Ball, when he'd kissed her. When she'd awakened in the middle of an old nightmare and thought he was Cole. And then again when she'd told him of the day her life had been torn to shreds by her own foolishness.

Did she have a right to hold him because he was everything she needed when she might never be what he needed?

"You awake?" he whispered into the still room.

She was tempted to play possum but knew the answer to her question had to be the opposite to the one he'd asked. No, she had no right to hold him. And since she was awake it was time to let him go. Time to be a better person than she'd ever been before.

"Yes. I'm awake. Why are you still here?"

"I told you I'd stay. You remember that, don't you?"

He sounded upset. Nearly panicked. Then she remembered the warning the doctor had given about the meaning of her becoming confused in the next several hours.

"Of course I remember. I just doubted you meant it, that's all," she said, tossing the remark off as cynically as she could manage while her heart already bled for his absence.

"Don't," he ordered, his voice stern but not the least bit annoyed.

"Don't what?" she asked, refusing to believe he could read her so easily. Surely he couldn't have figured out that quickly that she planned to drive him away.

"Don't try to push me away for my own good or some such nonsense."

She crossed her arms and looked away from him. "I don't know what you're talking about."

"Honey," he said, sitting on the ottoman next to her, "you are so transparent to me at this point that you don't have a prayer. I've been treated to the haughty act and swallowed it for a while. But then I met the real you. You've played the bad, loose woman, then admitted you'd lied. I've seen you act the snotty society deb with Cole about CJ, then watched you smile when he made a beeline for her to prove that he wasn't ashamed of her. You have to have gone through your entire repertoire with me already. I'm still here and not budging. Now, you want to tell me what this is all about or did I guess it?"

Elizabeth fought a trembling lip for a few seconds before she could say anything. "I keep hurting you. And I don't know if I'll ever be able to—" She stopped. She couldn't talk that frankly about sex with him. Not even after telling him about the rape.

"Let's get something straight," he said. "Right now, I just want your company. I want to get to know you. Explore my feelings for you and yours for me. If and when I want more, I'll ask. And I'll be asking for a lot more than a few hasty minutes in the sack. I've waited thirty-two years for that particular pleasure, and I reckon I can wait for a few more if necessary until you're ready for the question and all it entails. Understand?"

Elizabeth just stared at him. *I guess he told me.* She opened her mouth to make some rejoinder then closed it. Words escaped her when she saw the no-nonsense look in his eyes.

He gave her a sharp nod—the one she was coming to think of as his cowboy nod—and said, "Glad you got my point. Dinner's ready. I'll get it on the table if you're up to eating in the kitchen."

She watched him leave and swung her feet to the floor contemplating what he'd just said. "I've waited thirty-two years for that particular pleasure..." The man had to be the closest thing to an angel this side of heaven.

Chapter Sixteen

Jackson heard Beth shuffle into the kitchen behind him. He wondered if she'd continue trying to blind-side him with what, to someone who didn't know her, looked like a split personality. Or would she give up trying to push him away for his own good? He hoped she gave up, because his heart had just about stopped when she'd reverted to using that society-witch face she showed the people of her upper-crust world. But then he'd remembered that she didn't belong in that world, and her performance had become apparent.

He moved to the refrigerator and opened it, calling over his shoulder, "I tossed together a couple ome-lettes, and you had a roll of ready-to-bake biscuits in the fridge so I made them, too. You want jam, jelly, preserves, strawberry, cherry, tomato—" He stopped, staring at a full shelf of every spread available in the known world. "Beth, you either have a wicked sweet tooth or you're running a jelly museum in here."

When she made no reply to his joke, Jackson turned to her and was in motion in a nanosecond. She stood gripping the back of the chair, a river of tears flowing across her cheeks. He put an arm around her shoulder, feeling awkward and ineffective. "What is it, Beth?"

"It's been years since anyone took care of me. I've been alone with all of this bottled up inside me for so long."

Okay, so she'd inadvertently broken his heart a second time in one day. But that was okay. He was a big boy. He could take it. She'd lived a difficult, lonely life, and he wanted badly to rescue her from it, but he knew it was too soon.

Lord, give me the words to comfort her but don't let me push her too far too fast.

He sighed. "Well, you aren't alone anymore," he said and grabbed a napkin to blot her tears. "I'm honored to take care of you, honey. Why don't you sit down?"

Going on one knee in front of her, he patted her cheeks dry and looked her right in the eyes, willing her to believe him. "It's going to be all right."

Jackson wanted to say more. He wanted to sweep her up in his arms and take her to the Circle A where she could ride like the wind and leave the bad memories behind. But there were good things in her life she'd have to leave behind if he did that. And now that he thought about it, he'd be leaving almost as much behind as she would. It was a dilemma he wasn't looking forward to dealing with.

A quote from Philippians his pastor always used came back to him, and he silently recited it from memory. *In everything, by prayer and supplication with thanksgiving, let your requests be made known unto God. And the peace of God which passes all understanding shall keep your hearts and minds through Christ Jesus.*

He nearly smiled as that peace seeped into his soul. It didn't matter where they lived. If they were together, wherever they were would be home. He was sure of it.

On this trip to find his true roots, Jackson had learned home was a comfortable place of love and acceptance. He hoped it was a lesson Beth would learn, too. He hoped it was a lesson she was *able* to learn, because it looked as if Beth had never had a real home.

"How can you be so sure?" Beth asked, sniffling delicately.

"That everything will work out? Because God uses all things for good. Even the bad things."

"I don't understand. How can He use what Jason did to me for anything good? It was so evil."

He thought for a moment. "I'm not sure," he told her honestly. "That's a question you'll have to answer for yourself since I didn't know you before it happened."

She looked heartbreakingly sad. "It's hard for me to even remember what I was like before."

Jackson looked at the floor and searched for the right words. When he looked into her beautiful eyes he saw a yearning he'd never seen before and knew she desperately needed hope for the future. He was nearly certain the only way she'd ever have it was to go back and heal the child she'd been. To get to know that child again.

"Ask yourself if you would be the same kind of person you are now if none of the pain and heartbreak of the past had ever happened. If you hadn't felt betrayed by your parents, would you have swallowed their social line of garbage and become like them? Let's face it, you were destined to be a beauty even though everyone was too shortsighted to see it. Maybe you would have been as bad as those Lexington women if you hadn't faced such terrible adversity. As it is, you're a compassionate, kind, empathetic woman. You've gone out of your way to help other women who've felt the same loss of control over their lives that you've felt."

"You talk about me as if I were some sort of paragon of virtue instead of someone who lost her virtue years ago."

"That isn't true. You had your innocence stolen, but you can only lose your virtue if you choose to live an immoral life. From where I'm sitting, you haven't done that. Listen, I talked to Jim Dillon earlier. His wife, Holly, counsels the women of his church with personal problems. Would you consider talking to her about what happened in your past? I know turning to God for help is your answer. But I don't feel qualified to help you understand how He can make you feel like a new person and take away all your feelings of unworthiness. I do know the Bible tells us that all things are made new through Christ Jesus. And I know that He's never failed me.''

Her smile was faint, but at least it was there. ''That's good enough for me,'' she said. ''If you think Holly Dillon can help, I'll—I'll try to talk to her.''

''If tomorrow wouldn't be too soon, I could give her a call. We got a call that Hobart was denied bail, so if Holly could come here to talk to you in the morning, I won't worry you're alone.''

''You don't have to worry. I'll—''

''Be fine. I know, honey. But I won't be unless I'm sure you have someone with you for at least the morning.''

She smiled, and Jackson felt as if the sun had suddenly burst through the clouds.

''Jack, I don't know how I'll ever repay you for all you've done.''

He wanted to tell her that seeing her healed and ready to move ahead with a full and normal life as his wife would be repayment enough, but he settled for saying, ''Your pretty smile just did.''

Elizabeth heard voices. She opened her eyes and looked around. She was tucked into her fairy-tale, four-poster bed, and the shades and draperies were drawn against the morning light. But they were fighting a losing battle.

She easily identified Jack as one of the people speaking in hushed tones on the other side of her cozy little bedroom. Hearing that voice gave her such a warm secure feeling tears once again sprang to her eyes. The other voice was female, so she assumed Holly Dillon had already arrived.

Elizabeth wasn't sure she was ready to face a near stranger with the story of her regret and shame, but she also recognized the necessity of it. It was time to confront her feelings of unworthiness and fear if she wanted the chance to wake up for the rest of her life hearing Jack's voice nearby. And if there was one thing she was sure of, it was that she wanted the chance of a future with Jack.

A quiet knock on her door told Elizabeth it was time to find the courage she needed. When Jack moved silently into the room and came into view, she knew she had it. For him she would face Holly Dillon's censure and find a way to deal with her past. It was the path to fulfilling her childhood dreams of a family and a husband as different from her father as possible.

She'd forgotten those dreams. Then last night, in the quiet moments before sleep, she'd forced herself to remember the little girl who'd hugged and cared for her baby dolls as if they were real live offspring and who'd greeted her pretend husband at the door with a smile and a kiss.

Later, as life made those dreams more difficult for her to believe in, she'd still held out hope that her mythical childhood mate would one day ride out of the sunset, see her inner beauty and grant her every wish. It had been that hope and dream that had kept her going when the rest of the world saw only her flaws.

In adolescence, Elizabeth lost sight of those wishes and hopes when Jason Lexington showed her a side of human nature that had fractured her ability to trust any man. Her father's perfidy had followed and dealt trust a death blow.

But, little by little, Jack had changed that. She knew she still had a long way to go, but she could see a light at the end of the lonely tunnel of her life. And she knew if she could just reach it, Jack and happiness would be waiting. She prayed she didn't take too long to get there.

"Beth," Jack whispered, looking at her as if she were his world and he feared she might crumble at any moment. "You don't have to get up. I just wanted you to know I'm heading over to Laurel Glen. Holly Dillon's here but she's happy to just read while you sleep."

"No. I'm awake," she said and pushed the hair out of her eyes as she sat up. "Would you tell her before you leave that I'll be out in a minute? And please, try not to worry. I'll be fine."

He nodded, though the expression on his face told his real answer. He didn't intend to try very hard.

Holly Dillon was about five and a half feet tall with thick auburn hair, curling to her shoulders. In her early thirties, she hardly seemed like the person Elizabeth would have picked to confide in, but then again, the man she wanted to be free to love hadn't been her first pick for a confidant, either, and he'd been wonderful.

The smell of freshly baked biscuits and the subtle fragrance of brewing tea greeted Elizabeth as she entered her kitchen. The sight of Holly's smile as she looked up from spreading the freshly baked biscuits with a golden substance gave Elizabeth a warm feeling. Maybe this woman wouldn't be so hard to talk to, after all.

"Good morning, Elizabeth. Or should I call you Beth as Jack seems to?"

"Either is fine, Holly," she said, automatically agreeable, then she thought of Jack and his acceptance of her past. "Maybe Beth would be better. Maybe if I try hard enough, I can leave Elizabeth and her memories behind."

"You know you have to face those memories first and put them into the right perspective."

Elizabeth didn't know how she felt about him telling Holly Dillon about her past. Relieved that she didn't have to say the words once again? Disappointed that he hadn't kept her confidence?

"Jack *told* you?" she asked still not sure what answer she wanted to hear.

Holly shook her head. "Nothing specific. He said you needed someone to help you deal with something that happened in your early teen years. He felt you needed a woman to help you, and he thought that woman should be a Christian so you would get a God-centered perspective on your past and your future."

Elizabeth pulled a chair out and sat, still unsure of

the emotions that were suddenly bouncing all over the place. "That's just about what he said to me, but I confess I don't see that it matters."

Holly put a cup of tea and the golden biscuits in front of Elizabeth, then returned to the table with her own on a tray. On the tray were also two jars of jelly. "Both of these spreads are made with lemon," Holly said. "But the one I gave you is called lemon curd. Not a pretty name, but wonderful all the same. Both are lemon and both taste lovely. But they do taste different, and different ingredients went into them. Some people like one kind more than the other. It's the same with advice. Some advice and outlooks on life fit one person and others are better for different folks."

"Different strokes for different folks," Elizabeth said.

"Exactly. You've been coming to church with Meg Taggert, and it appears Jack is interested in you. Are you interested in him? Romantically, I mean."

Unsure if she could reveal something so personal after years of hiding her true self from most people, Elizabeth hesitated. It was the kindness she saw in Holly Dillon's eyes that finally gave her the courage to admit the truth. "I want to be. I guess I *am,* though it is a new experience for me."

"Is that why you've been coming to church?"

Elizabeth was startled by the abrupt candid question. "No. I was barely on speaking terms with Jack when I accepted Meg's invitation. I was as surprised to see him there as he was to see me."

"That's good. You were already seeking God."

"Why did you ask that?"

"You would be surprised how many young women and men come to church looking for a date. They are often insincere about their belief system, and others are hurt."

Elizabeth thought for a long moment. She'd told herself she'd gone with Meg because she was seeking answers, but now she knew it had been more. "Inside. I feel…hollow. As if there's this big empty spot nothing will ever fill. And I feel dirty because of what happened."

Holly smiled knowingly. "Hmm. Hollow is His specialty. He'd love to fill up that space for you with His love and peace. All you have to do is ask Him. But why dirty? You feel you've sinned?"

Elizabeth nodded and forged ahead. "When I was fourteen, I went off alone with an older boy. A young man, really. He was handsome and popular. He seemed kind and he flattered me. Then when we were too far away for anyone to hear me, he attacked me. He raped me."

Holly didn't even blink. "That was his sin, Beth. Not yours."

"That's what Jack says, but—"

"But you feel responsible all the same."

"I shouldn't have gone off with him. I should have seen what he was really like. It's what my parents thought."

"Do you feel responsible because you *were* responsible? Or is it that by accepting responsibility you keep control over what happened that day? And does that give you control over your future?"

"Control?"

"If someone says to themselves, 'I could have helped what happened,' they maintain control over an important aspect of their life. If they admit it was the fault of someone else, they've lost that control and have to admit it could happen again."

Elizabeth thought she understood. She even thought Holly might be right. "It did happen again. Didn't it?"

Holly nodded. "Jack did tell me about how Brian Hobart attacked you. That was about violence, and so was that boy's attack when you were younger."

"Jack said that, too."

"He's very wise, your Jack."

"I wish he could be. *My* Jack, I mean."

Holly eyed her with a knowing look. "But you feel too dirty for someone so fine. Is that it?"

"How can he look at me and not see what Jason did?"

"They say love is blind, so believe me, you have nothing to worry about where Jack is concerned. It's how you feel we need to fix. First, I want you to understand that feeling this way isn't what God our Father wants for you. In II Corinthians 5:17 Paul says, 'Therefore, if anyone is in Christ, he is a new creation; old things have passed away; behold, all things have become new.'"

Elizabeth felt as if light had suddenly dawned.

"That's why I went with Meg. I wanted God to make me feel better. Clean again."

Holly covered Elizabeth's hand with hers. "Then you came to the right place, dearie."

"But I still don't understand how I'm supposed to make it happen. I went twice and I felt better while I was there but I was still the same afterward."

"It's sort of a partnership. You and Jesus. And you have to do something first. You have to ask Him for help. You have to ask Him into your heart. You have to ask forgiveness for any past sins. You have to ask for healing. The rest is up to Him."

"That's all?" Elizabeth asked, skeptical. "It sounds too easy."

Holly's expression was grave. "You have to really believe, Beth. And it's not a decision to take lightly because once you make it you'll start seeing the world differently. Things you accepted as the way things are will bother you. He'll take over your life."

"That's why Jack is so different from other men I've met. Right?"

Holly nodded.

"He isn't the way I always assumed a Christian man would be," Elizabeth told Holly, feeling a sudden blush heat her face. What if the other woman asked what she meant? She would have to insult Holly's husband to explain.

Instead of asking or taking offense, Holly chuckled. "You thought Christian men were wimpy? Not hero material?"

Relieved, Elizabeth nodded and went on to explain.

"I was shocked when Jeff Carrington and then Ross Taggert started going to church. They're both strong men. Like Jack."

"Like Jesus," Holly reminded her. "Carpenters in His day had to chop down the tree they built with, and the day of the chain saw was a long way off. I don't think Jesus was a lightweight."

"Yesterday Jack was so angry when he got to where Brian Hobart had run me off the road. The police told me Jack had already subdued him when they arrived. Do you think I caused Jack to sin?"

Holly's ready smile turned gentle. "There's nothing wrong with righteous anger. Remember while Jesus did say to turn the other cheek, He also emptied the temple of the money changers. And none too gently, either." Her expression grew serious. "And remember something else. Though under God we have rights, along with every one of those rights comes a responsibility. You're allowed to be angry but you must forgive. You must admit more than that your assailant was responsible, in order to free you of guilt. You must also face your loss of control and give it into the Lord's hands."

"He would have to do a better job than I have," Elizabeth muttered.

Again Holly's gentle smile warmed her even as the other woman continued her instruction. "You have to let the Lord cleanse your soul and therefore your body. You can't metaphorically give Him the dirt you feel soils you with one hand while snatching it back with the other. You have to lay it all at His feet and walk away whole and cleansed. A new person in Christ. Can you do that for yourself, Beth?''

After Holly Dillon left, Elizabeth thought long and hard about their conversation and her earlier one with Jack about God and faith. She looked up several passages in the Bible Holly had brought for her, but none touched her soul the way that one from Corinthians did. She wanted all the things that verse and Holly and Jack had talked about. And she was ready to face the responsibilities Holly warned her she must.

In the solitude of her little home, Elizabeth prayed the prayer for salvation Holly had outlined for her, and while she didn't hear angels singing and strumming their metaphorical harps, she did feel an inner peace and a sense of belonging that she hadn't known since early childhood.

On Sunday morning Elizabeth intended to walk forward and respond if Jim Dillon gave an altar call. Elizabeth knew putting her faith in the Almighty wasn't a panacea for all her issues. In fact, she and Holly had a lunch date set for Monday so she could begin to work through her problem with trust and her fear of intimacy. But she felt as if she was on the right path at last.

Chapter Seventeen

Jackson arrived at Beth's door Saturday morning still surprised that she intended to keep their Philadelphia sight-seeing date so soon after Hobart's attack. He didn't want her pushing herself too far for his sake, even though it was a beautiful day for sight-seeing. The day was bright, the forecast was for lower than normal temperatures, and Beth greeted him with a smile so radiant it put the bright sun to shame.

"I was going to ask if you're sure you're up to this but I guess I shouldn't bother," he told her, gazing into her bottle-green eyes, transfixed by the happiness he saw reflected there.

"I'm a little stiff but my head isn't hurting at all now. Other than the cuts from the glass, I'm nearly good as new," she promised. "And I have a surprise. I thought we could do a little poking through history on the way to the city. It's less than a direct route but it's beautiful there."

Jackson gestured toward the truck. "Your chariot awaits, ma'am."

"Why, thank you, kind sir. First stop Valley Forge Park," she continued when he slid in beside her after closing her door.

Beth was a woman of her word. She directed him into the picturesque national park nearly an hour later, and his Colorado soul found a spot among the rolling Pennsylvania hills to call his own. Valley Forge Mountain might not be the kind of mountain he was used to but it did provide an incredible view of the countryside below.

"I'd say General Washington chose well that winter," he said as he stood on the promontory and looked over the deep valley. "Nobody was getting up here without him knowing about it."

Beth's smile lit the day even brighter. "I thought you'd like it up here." She pointed behind them then off to the left. "Those are the redoubt forts the Colonials dug, but thankfully they never had to use them. We can go see a few of the cabins next, then circle back to the tourist center. They've put a lot of the equipment and weapons the Colonials used on display in there. And there's also Washington's headquarters to see."

"Well, what are we waiting for?" he asked as he watched a father help his sons launch an oversize kite. The lightweight fabric craft rose into the sky and joined a variety of others that flew against a backdrop of a cloud-studded blue sky.

Two hours later they were on their way to the city.

Jackson already had a greater sense of the nation's history than all the textbooks he'd ever read and all the lectures he'd ever listened to had given him. The men had lived through that harsh winter in crude log cabins, many starving to death or dying of disease for the noble cause of unprecedented freedom.

Washington's headquarters had been older than any building Jackson had ever seen, dating from the early part of the eighteenth century. And the best was yet to come.

Once in Philadelphia they ate lunch on the run bought from sidewalk vendor carts—hot dogs and sauerkraut slathered with spicy mustard and a salty soft pretzel topped with a traditional coat of yellow mustard. Both were a must, according to Beth. Jackson, wanting to steep himself in her environment, went along with her every suggestion and was glad of it.

They saw the Liberty Bell in what she called its ''new'' pavilion, though he learned the bell had been moved there from its traditional home in Independence Hall in 1976 for the increased traffic the Bicentennial brought to the city. He guessed when a city had over three hundred years of history, the twenty-five-year-old pavilion would be considered a new addition. And now plans were being put forward to move it again to increase security.

Next they moved to Independence Hall. At first its steeple had Jackson thinking they were approaching a church from across Independence Hall. But then he took in the whole building, and the pictures he'd seen of Independence Hall came to life. Jackson left knowing he'd seen the place where liberty was born.

For the next four hours, Beth, the park guards and tour guides brought the history he loved so much to life. One of the places that stood out from others was Carpenters' Hall, a beautifully constructed artisans' meetinghouse that had once housed the First Continental Congress.

They sat and had a cool drink at City Tavern where the first and second Congressional delegates often met. Next they visited Old Saint Joseph's Church where legend holds that local Quakers surrounded their fellow Philadelphians to keep them safe from an angry mob in defense of liberty and their right to worship in the Catholic tradition as they saw fit.

On their way to Elfreth's Alley, he and Beth came upon the Betsy Ross house, where tradition said the nation's first official flag was sewn. Jackson was fascinated by Elfreth's Alley when they reached it. It was a perfectly preserved street of privately owned Colonial homes, and their journey felt more like a three-hundred-year step back in time than part of a modern-day walking tour.

By then his stomach was shaking hands with his backbone and his feet had had about all they could take of concrete pavements. He hadn't heeded Beth's warning and had worn his boots, eschewing what she called sneakers and back home they called tennis shoes. Beth pretended to be unsympathetic, but she laughingly took pity on him. She soon had them in the heart of Chinatown and sitting in a wonderful Asian restaurant.

He found a steak on the menu, and Beth ordered a sushi sampler. It wasn't long before he was ordering another sampler for them to share since he'd eaten half the raw fish delicacies off Beth's plate. And he'd been so sure he could never get even a bite of one down.

It was a full and wonderful day, and Beth was still teasing him about his steak doggie bag when they got to her little carriage house well after dark. They'd no sooner gained her cozy parlor when someone pounded on the door at the bottom of the steps they'd just mounted.

Hoping Hobart somehow hadn't found a sympathetic judge, Jackson frowned. "I'll get that while you take care of serving up that coffee you promised to go with these Italian pastries you walked my feet off to get. You plumb wore this cowboy out today, little lady," he teased, seeing her worry as she peered toward the door where the insistent knocking sounded again.

"I'll get it," he told her again, and went to the door.

Jackson was surprised to see her parents standing on the other side of the door when he lifted the curtain aside. The mutinous expressions on their faces had him wishing he was only facing a furious Brian Hobart again. Determined to ease troubled waters, he pasted on an attempt at a smile and quickly opened the door.

"Mr. Boyer. Mrs. Boyer. Beth was just about to make us some coffee to go with some pastries we picked up in Philadelphia today. Come on in. There's plenty to go around."

The bottom of the stairs afforded only a small foyer that wasn't big enough for three, so Jackson turned and led the way up the steps, calling a request for Mr. Boyer to close and lock the door.

Jackson heard Reginald Boyer grumble, "Nervy upstart."

"You can relax, Beth," he called toward the kitchen. "It's your parents." He knew the news was more than likely no less unwelcome for her than it had been for him. "Why don't you make a few extra cups of coffee?" he continued in the same conciliatory vein he'd adopted with the middle-aged couple.

"See here. We didn't come here to socialize with the likes of you," Reginald Boyer blustered.

"Then what did you come here for, Father?" Beth demanded as she stepped out of the kitchen. "I believe this is a first. Mother usually calls me to come up to the big house when she feels the need to connect with me."

"If you wouldn't choose to live in the servants' quarters, I wouldn't make myself so scarce. As for why we came here, after that last visit, I assumed you would ignore my invitation," Louise Boyer said, nose in the air as if she smelled something offensive.

Jackson was tempted to check his boots but knew it was his presence she found so disagreeable.

"You would have been right," Beth agreed.

"What did you want to talk to me about that was so urgent you broke precedent to come to the servants' quarters?"

"Your father intends to close the deal on this portion of land in a day or so. We came here today to warn you that you'll have to move back into our house soon. And just so there is no misunderstanding, *he* will not be welcome."

There was no question who *he* was.

Beth didn't blink. She'd clearly been weighing her options all along. Calmly, as if inviting her parents to tea, she warned, "Try selling to that developer, and I'll take you to court. I'll let everyone know what you did with Maggie's pension, why I live here and why I don't feel I can afford to live anywhere else."

"You wouldn't do that to your own father."

"Don't bet the farm, Father," Beth said, never flinching. "It wouldn't be a wise investment."

Her father looked dumbstruck but Louise Boyer was clearheaded enough to go on the attack. "What has happened to you? We know all about that incident yesterday. This simply cannot go on. Your association with that horrid group of women is bound to get out. Can you imagine the scandal if it becomes general knowledge that you consort with the homeless every day?"

Beth's jaw hardened. "The women at the New Life Inn are homeless through no fault of their own. And the man who attacked me yesterday was driving a sixty-thousand-dollar luxury car. *He* was the lowlife, not his poor frightened wife."

"And I want to know what *this* lowlife is doing here on my property," Reginald Boyer demanded, coming out of his stupor on the attack.

Gritting his teeth, Jackson moved toward the stairway, not wanting to make this scene worse for Beth and thinking if he left she might be able to salvage some sort of relationship with her family. "I'll give you a call—"

"Jack Alton, don't you dare move a muscle!" Beth ordered, then turned furious eyes on her parents. "This man is my friend."

"What on earth does he have to recommend him? Cole Taggert was bad enough with his past but at least he's from an old respected family. This…this cowboy is only Laurel Glen's foreman, for pity's sake," Mr. Boyer snarled with a sideways look that might well have struck Jackson dead if such a thing were possible.

"He cares about me, and I care about him. What else he has to recommend him is that he's a good, God-fearing man who more than likely saved my life yesterday."

"Don't be melodramatic, Elizabeth. It doesn't become you," Louise Boyer snapped, crossing her arms and stiffening her shoulders.

"Elizabeth, your mother's just worried you've trusted the wrong man again. You admit you did exactly this once before and nearly brought disaster down on our heads."

"Well, now, that kind of tears it," Jackson said, moving from the stairs to stand next to Beth. "I was determined to keep my peace and not annoy either of you since you're Beth's parents. But now I see my mistake. I'd heard it takes more than biology to make a parent, and you two could be poster children for the idea.

"You were both so worried about your standing in the community that you sacrificed years of your daughter's peace of mind and happiness with your self-centered rhetoric. A monster kidnapped and raped your little girl, and all you could do was blame her for being in the wrong place at the wrong time. Is every victim of crime at fault or just your child?"

"You can't talk to us like that," Reginald Boyer said.

"Someone needs to, and it might as well be me since I care about her. Something I'm not sure can be said of either of you."

Beth put a restraining hand on his forearm. "It's okay, Jack. I can handle this. Jack is more than welcome in my home and I'm saying it again—if you try to sell this carriage house out from under me, I'll take you to court and air our dirty laundry in public. And please know that I mean every word. Now, my friend and I were just about to have a nice cup of coffee and some pastries. You may either sit down and be civil or you may leave."

"Elizabeth, think of the scandal if it becomes known that he's living here with you. He isn't our kind."

"Now wait a minute, Mrs. Boyer." Jack ground the words out. "I am not living here and I'm insulted for both Beth and myself that you would assume such a thing. Yes, I stayed here Thursday night but only because Beth has a concussion. And, by the way, thank you so much for asking after your daughter's health, she's going to be fine.''

Beth seemed spellbound when her mother opened her mouth to respond to his newest indictment. Then a surprising thing happened. Louise Boyer blushed scarlet, turned and marched down the stairs and out the door. She returned for just a second. "Come along, Reginald. Elizabeth has made her decision.''

Without a blink of an eye, Beth's father turned and followed his wife out of the carriage house.

"And I always thought my father ruled the roost,'' Beth said.

"Apparently, honey, you were wrong. I'm sorry if you're annoyed that I spoke up. I couldn't keep my mouth shut. That crack about Lexington really frosted me.''

"It's okay. I'm not at all angry. Thank you for defending me. It's what they should have been doing all along. Isn't it?''

Jack nodded. There seemed nothing else to say so he hugged her.

"Let's have our coffee and try to put this behind us,'' she said, her suggestion muffled against his chest. "This won't change my life in the slightest. I see now that my parents have been nothing more than an annoyance to be dealt with for years. It's time I gave up trying to appease them.''

"But they are your parents. I don't want you having to choose me over them."

Beth stepped back from him and gifted him with a watery smile. "You don't mourn what you never had. They were never more than demanding guardians. You were right. They were never parents. I have a Father in heaven and I'm pretty sure He will do just fine for me now that I know I can go to Him for comfort and to ask His advice."

Such joy bloomed in Jackson's heart that he blinked back tears. He gathered her in his arms and swung her in a circle. "You understand! Praise the Lord!" he shouted and kissed her.

Chapter Eighteen

Elizabeth tried to shut out everything but Jack and his exuberant kiss, and she managed. He tasted of the chocolate bar he'd munched on the way home and the mint he'd picked up at the door of the restaurant. His unique male scent mingled in her mind with those things, and her mind labeled all those things *love*. His fingers combing her hair felt good, too, but then the good feelings began to slip away, just out of reach.

Like an ominous cloud suddenly obscuring the sun, Jack's strength and size abruptly overwhelmed her. She tried to draw in air, but her airway felt constricted. All at once she was fighting to breathe.

"It's okay," she heard Jack saying. "You have to know I'd never hurt you, Beth."

"I do know," she told him, but she felt as if she were speaking from far away. Then she blinked and looked into his sorrowful blue eyes. She didn't know when he'd set her down or how long he'd been kneeling before her, but she knew she trusted him. "But I'd hurt *you*. I just did."

He gifted her with a crooked smile, but still she saw that it was tinged with sadness. "I'm tough."

She put her hand over his heart. "Not here, you aren't. I don't know how to keep from hurting you. And I hate that he comes between us. Please believe that."

"I understand."

She shook her head. "I don't see how you can when I don't." And she couldn't go on hurting him. It was wrong. She couldn't stand to see the sorrow in his eyes each time she rejected a simple kiss. "I think maybe we shouldn't see each other anymore. I—"

"No." He ground the word out, silencing her with a gentle finger sealing her lips. "We aren't giving up the kind of joy we found today in each other's company because someone hurt you and damaged something inside you. We're going to work to repair that damage, and this is going to work out. We're going to fix it with God's help. I believe that. You have to, too. There's more to a good relationship than kissing. We'll work on those things together. Meanwhile, you'll work with Holly, and I'll keep my lips and my hands to myself."

"But I like it when you put your arms around me. Most of the time I feel safe. When you hug me when I'm sad, I feel this beautiful burst of happiness feeling you so close. It's just when you kiss me that I—" Elizabeth paused, thinking, trying to discern what had happened. "I don't even know what happens."

He sat on his heels and smiled. "Okay. Arms—good. Adding lips—bad. We'll figure out why. I'm not giving up. You aren't, either. Maybe once we start your self-defense lessons they'll help by making you feel less vulnerable to someone my size. I'm thinking it's some kind of automatic response that we need to change into something else."

"You really mean that? You really think I can learn to defend myself?"

Jack chuckled, his eyes alight with gentle affection. "My sister, Crystal, has been able to put me in the dirt since she was fifteen. We lived on a ranch and we couldn't always be sure of the extras we hired at roundup time. Even though Dad was careful, you can never be too cautious, so I took self-defense lessons with her. She learned how to take care of herself."

Feeling more confident, she smiled. "When do we start?"

"Not till I get my coffee and pastries."

"They're cannoli, and you have a hollow leg."

"Only one? Grandmother swore it was both of them."

"You're going to get fat, Jack Alton," she warned with a chuckle as he got lithely to his feet

Jack laughed. "Then there'll be more of me to love."

How could I love you any more? she thought, and stared at him for a long moment before going to get their dessert.

"You really do have two hollow legs," Elizabeth told Jack after watching him devour three cannoli—

one chocolate cream, one vanilla cream and one chocolate chip and ricotta cheese.

"Maybe that's why you were nearly able to walk them off today."

"Maybe if you'd listened about wearing the sneakers," she teased.

Jack stood to help her remove the dishes. He'd pulled his boots off, but he still towered over her. "So are you ready for your first lesson?" he asked, setting the tray he carried on the kitchen counter next to the sink.

Elizabeth looked at him. "This is silly. There's no way—"

"Uh-uh. There's no room in my classroom for a doubter. And once you see the way this works you'll understand. The first thing I want to work on is what to do if someone gets a choke hold on your throat. You told me that Lexington tried to choke you, and you seemed to think you couldn't breathe earlier."

Her heart started pounding. Now that he mentioned it, she did remember fighting for breath.

"Calm down," he said, reading her change of mood perfectly. "I'm the one who's going to get choked first." He sat in a chair with his back to her. "This should even us up some. I want you to try to choke me."

"You're kidding, right?"

He turned and looked at her. "I'm deadly serious, honey. And I promise, at first I won't use a bit of strength to defend myself."

She grimaced. "I'm not sure I like that any better. What if I hurt you?"

"You won't. Now come on. Give it your best shot."

Reluctantly she put her hands around his neck.

"Come on, Beth. Like you mean it. Remember how obnoxious I was when we first met?"

That didn't make it any easier, but she did exert pressure as ordered. And that's when he surprised her by pushing his fingers then hands, palms out, under her fingers. She pressed harder, carefully at first then with even more pressure.

"You said you wouldn't use your strength," she complained and dropped her hands.

"Bloodthirsty little thing you're turning out to be. All I did was get my hands between yours and my neck. I was just holding them there. No strength at all. As long as my hands are there in that way you can't choke me. Try again, and I'll show you how to break an assailant's hold."

They worked for about fifteen minutes. He showed her how to use the way the body is formed against someone trying to subdue her with a choke hold. It was so logical an approach she didn't know why it wasn't taught to every young girl in school.

As he was leaving, Jack turned at the door, and she knew he was wishing for a kiss good-night. He looked as lonely as she felt.

"I'll pick you up at nine for church. Sweet dreams," he said and turned to leave.

But she laid a restraining hand on his arm and

leaned forward from her perch in the doorway to plant a quick peck on his slightly whiskered cheek. "You have sweet dreams, too, Jack Alton."

He touched her lips with his fingertips and stepped back, saying not a word, but she saw him cover his cheek for a second when he got in the truck. Then he shook his head, started his pickup and drove off down her lane.

Jackson looked next to him at Beth, and his heart once again swelled with pride. He thanked the Lord for her salvation. It had been a touching moment at the service earlier when she'd gone forward and Holly Dillon had gotten up to hug her, shedding a generous amount of tears. His mother had shed enough tears to float a boat herself, especially when Cole Taggert had joined Beth at the front of the church to rededicate himself to the Lord he'd turned his back on years ago.

For a few minutes there, Jackson had been a bit worried that Cole's presence at Beth's side was more than a coincidence. But then after Jim Dillon led them all in a public prayer, Cole had turned to Beth, and after a few words, he'd returned to CJ Larson's side for a congratulatory hug and kiss. The two were obviously in love, and Jackson was able to relax before meeting Beth halfway up the aisle. Her smile had been beatific when she reached him.

I love you. The words were on the tip of his tongue but he managed to hold back, not wanting to burden her with the weight of his feeling. Beth was wrestling with enough guilt over her fears already.

He'd planned another self-defense lesson for that day, wanting Beth to work on the same move but with him acting as the aggressor this time. He knew the best approach was to give her a feeling of control at the same time Holly was working to show her that Jason Lexington had taken control from her.

Jack had visited a Web site on self-defense and had gotten several tips that gave women more control by teaching them warning signs of dangerous situations and aggressive men. It would be so easy to pledge to always be there for Beth, but that would take her from one prison to another. And his love was all about giving her freedom.

Freedom from fear. Freedom from loneliness. Freedom from the need to hide her real self behind a perfect facade.

Freedom to love.

His lessons and plans would have to wait, though, because Meg had invited them to Laurel House for a lunch celebrating Laurel Glen's recent blessings. Ross was home and was going to be fine. CJ's win at the Graystone Cross-country was already boosting business. Little Laurel Taggert, while she had the adult household in an uproar, stole the heart of anyone who came in contact with her. And Cole and Ross had reconciled after years of discord, with Cole turning his heart to the Lord as his father had nearly a year before.

Jackson hoped Meg intended to use this opportunity to announce his true relationship to her, but his mother had once again made a plea for patience. He understood her feelings and hadn't wanted to upset her, but he grew increasingly worried that Beth would feel he'd hidden a part of himself from her, especially after she'd shared her most intimate secrets with him. And he didn't see how he could tell his mother Beth had trust issues without revealing her secrets.

Talk about being between a rock and a hard place!

As he drove under the arch into Laurel Glen, Beth sighed next to him, drawing his attention to the problems he *could* deal with.

"What's wrong?" he asked her.

"Every time I come here I wish they were my family. Even with all the problems they've had, they still hang together."

"I've noticed you don't blame Ross for the rift between him and Cole."

"They were both at fault. Two headstrong men refusing to bend or talk about what happened between them. I just hope this isn't a temporary truce."

Jackson hesitated, wondering if he should tell her that Cole's arrest was still a large bone of contention between the two men. He guessed she had a right to know.

"There may be something you can do that would help their relationship."

Her eyes widened. "Me?"

Nodding, Jackson explained. "Cole continues to protect you, and Ross still believes he wasn't alone. I've heard them argue about it when they didn't know I was around."

Her forehead wrinkled adorably as she thought

about what he'd told her. "You think I should tell Cole he's free to explain?"

"It isn't fair to come between them, and I think you see that no good came of keeping what happened a secret."

Her shoulders slumped, and she laced her fingers together, staring at them for a long moment. "You're right. I've been so selfish."

"No. You were led to believe hiding the truth was the right thing to do, but it wasn't right for anyone. That was your parents' fault, not yours."

"If I get any time alone with Cole today, I'll tell him he's free to explain what happened that afternoon and later that night."

As it turned out, Cole was the first person they came upon at Laurel House. They'd entered the foyer when Jackson's near twin came bounding down the steps.

"Elizabeth," his cousin called. "The women are gathering in the nursery for a summit. At issue is Laurel and whether it's okay for her to suck her thumb."

"There's nothing wrong with thumb sucking. I did it."

"But you had braces," Cole reminded her. "There was enough metal on those teeth to set off metal detectors."

Beth put a defiant hand on her hip. "I'll have you know my dentist said it didn't have a thing to do with sucking my thumb. My mouth was just too small for my teeth!"

"And beautiful teeth they are," Cole said, gallantly bowing. "I guess you'd better run on up and cast your vote."

Beth turned to Jackson. "Do you mind?

He loved seeing her so relaxed. So happy. It was his main hope for her. "Go ahead. I'm sure Cole and I can find something to talk about."

She looked unsure. "I'll tell him what I decided. Okay?"

"Any way you want to handle it," Jackson agreed.

"You and my pal seem to be becoming an item," Cole said when Beth was out of earshot. He leaned indolently against the thick newel post at the foot of the impressive curved staircase. "Complete with a pet name and all. I've never heard anyone call her anything but Elizabeth."

Jackson knew when he was being baited. Cole still didn't trust him, and Jackson didn't blame him. Unfortunately, he was honor bound not to explain his presence. "She's Beth to me and she isn't complaining. In fact, she seems to like it," he replied as mildly as possible, trying not to rise to Cole's challenge.

"From her cryptic little statement just now, I gather there's an announcement in the offing. Don't hurt her, Alton. I know you have an ulterior motive for being here. I haven't figured it out yet, but there's something more to you than a new foreman who just suddenly turned up."

"Beth mentioned that you feel that way. I'm sorry you do. Please believe I'd die before hurting Beth.

She's had too much heartache in her life, thanks to Lexington and her parents.''

Cole's eyes widened. "She told you?" he asked, obviously incredulous. "She wouldn't even talk to me about it when I came home, and I already knew what happened. I assumed she'd mostly put it behind her."

Jackson shook his head. "I found out because on Thursday the husband of one of her clients ran Beth off Stoney Hollow Road, dragged her out of her car and assaulted her. I got to her not a minute after he smashed her windows to get to her, but she was shaken and confused from a concussion."

He paused, trying to blot out the memory of those minutes on the road when he'd been so terrified for her. "She thought I was you and it was…that other time," he continued. "I'll never be able to thank you enough for saving her that day."

Cole was clearly stunned. His lazy pose disintegrated, and he sank to the third step. "And I'm indebted to you for saving her on Thursday. But make no mistake, I protect what's mine. If you're here to make trouble for any member of this family or you hurt Elizabeth, you *will* answer to me."

Jack spread his hands. "I'm not here to cause anyone trouble. I give you my word."

"And how do I know what your word is worth?"

"What are you two so serious about?" Beth said as she started down the stairs.

"I was telling Cole about what Hobart pulled on Thursday," Jackson told her. Knowing he needed to leave her alone with Cole, he went on trying to hide his worry. "Listen, honey, I need to talk to Ross about a couple things down at the stables. Why don't you and Cole visit a while?"

Beth nodded, and Cole told him where Ross was. Jackson reluctantly turned to walk away, hoping Cole didn't make her suspicious of his motives again. He prayed he'd get the chance to tell her the truth about himself freely and not under a shadow of betrayal. And he wanted it for her sake as well as his own.

Chapter Nineteen

"So what's this big announcement?" Cole asked abruptly.

Elizabeth turned from watching Jack saunter off toward the sunroom. "Announcement?" she asked.

"This thing you told Alton you wanted to tell me yourself. You marrying the guy or something?"

"Oh." Elizabeth felt a blush heat her face. "There's no announcement. Jack and I haven't come quite that far yet. But I am hoping eventually…" She halted when Cole didn't smile as she'd thought he would. He'd always cared about her happiness. Didn't he see that Jack was the best thing to ever happen to her? That every waking minute was no longer haunted by the past?

"I hope you aren't making a mistake," he said, and sat on the steps where he'd been when she'd started downstairs. He might have appeared relaxed were his expression not so tense. "Something about that guy still doesn't add up," he continued, giving voice to his expression.

Elizabeth's heart fell, and she sank to the step below him. "You're wrong about Jack. I hate to insult you but you sound just like my parents."

Cole grinned. "Ouch."

"Really, he's exactly what he appears to be. A wonderful man who loves God and I hope me. He must, or I doubt he'd have been able to put up with me for even this long."

"There you go, selling yourself short again."

"That's not what I'm doing, Cole. The truth is I still sort of freak out when a man gets too close physically. Jack understands and he's helped me see a lot of what's happened in a new and clearer light. And regardless of your opinion of him, Jack suggested I release you from your promise."

"Promise?" Cole asked, frowning with obvious confusion.

She nodded. "The promise you made the day you saved me from Jason Lexington."

Cole's jaw hardened, and he pursed his lips. "A lot of good I did. If I'd walked out of that stupid class instead of waiting for dismissal, he wouldn't—" He broke off and looked away.

She reached out and put a hand on his knee. "Oh, no. You felt responsible, too? Cole, that's wrong. You saved my life. He had a knife and he'd have killed me if you hadn't followed us. I owe you a great debt. And as a reward I've forced you to carry this awful secret for me even though it hurt your relationship with your father. I'm sorry for that. I think you should explain to Ross what happened that day. I don't want to be the reason for a rift opening up between you two again.''

''But—''

She halted his protest with a sharp shake of her head. ''No buts. It's time to heal. For both of us. Talk to Ross. Tell him all of it.''

Silently he nodded and stood, offering her a hand up. ''I can't talk you into being more cautious where Alton's concerned?''

She sighed. ''Honestly, who needs a brother with a friend like you around?''

As if on cue a flurry of indignant yowls flowed down the stairs. Cole snorted. ''Yeah, and I didn't need another hardheaded sister, and now I probably have three, since I thought of you as a sister for years even though we didn't see each other,'' he groused as she took his hand and let him pull her to her feet. ''You'd better be right about Alton or I'm going to hand him his head.''

''You harm a hair on his head and I'll have yours.''

''Fight nice, dears,'' Meg Taggert said as she floated down the stairs. Her azure-blue and red caftan wafted in the breeze created by her lively stride. Hope Carrington once said her aunt Meg was the Auntie Mame of the county, and Elizabeth couldn't think of a more apt description of the forceful matriarch of the Taggert family.

''We weren't fighting, sweetheart,'' Cole said. ''I

was just making sure *Beth* here knows what she's doing.''

Meg smiled, but it seemed almost as if her eyes managed to frown. ''I'd count on it, darling boy.'' She stared at Elizabeth for a long moment. ''Beth. Yes. I think that's just about perfect.'' She clapped her hands. ''Now, let's join the men. Hope and Amelia will be down momentarily, and we can get this celebration moving. You're both drafted to carry the gifts.''

Cole rubbed his hands together. ''Gifts? Well, in that case, lead on. Nothing I like better than my aunt Meg's gifts.''

Still feeling a little strange to have been included in the Taggerts' day of celebration when she wasn't Cole's date but Jack's, Beth followed. She listened to Cole and Meg banter and felt a hunger deep in her spirit. She might wish she was a Taggert clan member, but she was ever mindful of her real place and of the pitiful state of her own family.

She hadn't heard from her parents after Jack left last night, and by midnight she'd realized she probably wouldn't. So she'd sat herself down and had written to her brother, Adam, through the Navy and the Red Cross, intending to extend a hand to him as Jack had suggested. But as she'd begun writing, memories of him had surfaced, and she'd found herself pouring out her heart to the big brother her parents had expelled from her life so many years ago. God willing, he wouldn't ignore her as her parents often did.

* * *

"Beth," Jack growled, hands on his hips and a look of exasperation wrinkling his forehead. "If you don't stop laughing this is never going to work."

"I'm sorry," she said as she flopped down on their picnic blanket. "I don't know what's wrong with me. It just struck me so funny. It's a ridiculous idea. Why would someone my size attack someone as big as you? How am I supposed to get my arms around you and pin them to your sides? My hands didn't even meet in the middle."

Jack dropped his head back and looked beseechingly heavenward at the clear mid-September sky. "You seeing what I put up with down here, Lord?" His hangdog, can't-get-no-respect expression sent Elizabeth into gales of laughter once again.

A few minutes later, after wiping her eyes of merry tears, she decided it was time to get serious and pushed herself to her feet. "Okay. Come on, Jack. Admit it. This is one move you have to show me with you as the aggressor." She turned her back to him. "Just grab me and tell me what to do."

He sighed, then wrapped his arms gently around her. "The first thing you do is stomp on my instep. Then when I'm off guard—and believe me, I would be because it hurts like blue blazes when someone stomps on your foot like that—you kick straight back at my knee. Keep your heel and toes flat and bring your calf parallel to the ground. That helps deliver maximum power and helps you keep your balance. Now try it in slow motion."

She did as he instructed, and they worked on the

self-defense move several times before they took a break to enjoy their picnic lunch. When they were done, Jack went to check on the horses, and Elizabeth walked to the top of the rise to look over the valley below.

It was her father's land, and the hill she'd just crested overlooked the main house and the old carriage house. Elizabeth had brought Jack to another of her special childhood places for a reason. As part of her work with Holly Dillon, Elizabeth tried to deal with a different troubling memory each day before giving the pain to God. Some days were more successful than others, and most were difficult. Today Holly had suggested she deal with her memories and loss of her brother, Adam. Elizabeth had been thinking about him so much lately, so she'd picked this place—the last place she'd seen her beloved brother.

Standing where they'd played together, she found it impossible to resist memories of the brother she'd been ordered to forget. She and Adam had often come here with Maggie O'Neill, her parents' housekeeper, who was really the closest thing to a mother either of them had ever had.

It had been a day much like this one, though it had been early summer and not early fall, when he'd followed her and Maggie there to explain that he was leaving. Elizabeth had been hateful in her pain, lashing out as only an injured, disappointed child can. She remembered that little girl with unusual clarity, and much of her guilt fled. She *had* been but a child.

She could admit her unanswered letters to him were

beginning to hurt. She usually forced her mind onto other things when she grew impatient for news. Or she told herself it had been only a month. That the Red Cross and the Navy had more important things to do these days than to spend a lot of time tracking down one sailor.

Jack had a different take. He wondered if her brother was in the Navy anymore. Seventeen years, he'd pointed out, was a long time.

Without warning a man wrapped his arms around her from behind, and Elizabeth did exactly as Jack had instructed. She stomped down hard on the foot just behind hers. At the sound of Jack's howl of pain, she managed to check her kick to his knee, giving it only a glancing blow. She whirled to face him as soon as he let go of her.

"Why would you sneak up on me that way? I could have really hurt you."

He limped to a nearby boulder and pulled off his boot, then rubbed his injured foot. "No could have about it," he said as he blinked against the pain. "You caught me a good one. Didn't you hear me say it was time to get back to work?"

"My mind was somewhere else. I'm so sorry. Did I hurt you very badly?"

Jack grinned. "Hurts pretty bad. But, hey, that's great. Let me tell you," he went on, still rubbing his instep, "if I'd been a real assailant and that kick to my knee had landed the way you originally intended, I'd have been on the ground howling and you would have had the chance to run."

His grin faded, and his expression turned serious. "Running is the one thing I want you to always keep in mind no matter how good at this you get. Fleeing danger is always the best weapon. Another is not second guessing a bad feeling. Think of it as God whispering a warning in your ear. According to the experts, women too often become victims because they don't want to make waves. The worst that can happen if you act is you look foolish. No one's ever been physically hurt or died of embarrassment, so far as I've ever heard."

"That's what I did that day. When I got that first funny feeling about Jason Lexington, I should have run. You can be sure I'll never second guess myself again."

"Good. Now come give me a hug," he demanded, grinning broadly. "I'm feeling mighty mistreated right now."

Without a second's thought she threw herself into his strong embrace, and for the first time no ominous cloud descended on her mind when his lips met hers. She supposed it was a chaste kiss by many standards, but to Elizabeth it was a miracle and a wonder. And when Jack lifted his head after a few magical seconds, she saw that it was clearly a moving experience for him, as well.

"Oh, honey," he breathed against her lips, his voice a little rough and his grin a little shaken. "You might have taken a while to get here, but you pack one whale of a punch now. Let's go have some of that pie and forget the lessons for today. I think it's time we celebrated a little.''

Jack might have been willing to take the afternoon off but Elizabeth wasn't. He'd taught her quite a bit so far about keeping herself safe, and she'd found that with her knowledge of self-defense increasing, so was her confidence as she went about her days. So after they had their pie, she idly asked how his foot felt now that he'd had ice on it for several minutes.

''It's just a little uncomfortable. I'll be able to put my boots back on just fine.''

''Are you up to showing me that other self-defense move you talked about? The one to ward off a frontal attack?''

He frowned. ''You're sure? I don't want to overwhelm you with this stuff.''

''I trust you, Jack. And I promise to let you know if and when I feel overwhelmed. I'm not made of spun glass.''

He leaned forward and kissed her cheek. ''How about spun sugar?''

She pushed herself to her feet. ''Oh, ho. Now he tries sweet talk. Let's go, lazy bones, or is it fraidy cat?''

Jack got to his feet, as well. ''It's another leverage move. Face me,'' he ordered. ''If someone comes at you from the front you grab his wrists. Or just one.'' He took her wrist. ''Point your index finger and push. Wherever you point your finger that's where his hand will go when you push his hand away.''

He demonstrated and then had her allow him to

grab her. She pointed her finger, but in a way that brought her lips within a hairbreadth of his. Jack froze, and she gazed into his blue eyes. They were suddenly intensely lit from within, and she could see his desire for her. Each of them ended the mock combat as if they were of one mind, and he wrapped her in his embrace. It was thrilling. Profoundly intimate. And when he kissed her, it was awe-inspiringly beautiful.

He broke the kiss several long moments later. "And that is why I thought we should forget the lessons for today. I just don't seem to be able to touch you and not want more. You understand, honey?"

"I not only understand. I think I feel the same way."

"Oh, now I know we had better head on back."

He set her gently away and went to put on his boots. His response worried Elizabeth, and she guessed that worry showed because Jack turned to her and asked, "Confused?"

She nodded.

That's when he grinned ruefully. "It isn't that I don't want to go on kissing you. But too much of a good thing can be a little painful and sometimes downright dangerous."

She blushed and turned to start packing up the lunch. "I guess maybe we *should* go back."

"I know so, honey. At times like this there's safety in numbers. Besides, aren't you curious whether Hope's labor was false again or if this time she finally had that baby?"

She nodded, and when they reached Laurel Glen's working hub they saw a new bunch of pink balloons had been tied outside the stall of Cobby, the thirty-year-old Welsh cob pony Cole and Hope had ridden as children.

"I imagine it's a girl! I'm going up to talk to Amelia and get all the particulars," she told him, and handed him Glory's reins. Then she stopped, a look of chagrin crossing her face. "Oh, I'm sorry. I should help stable her."

"Beth, it's me who's sorry. I didn't realize you pay for those services when I opened my big mouth that day I yelled at you for jumping the fence. You run along and bring back good news. I'll handle Glory."

She put her hand on his shoulder. "No. Really. I want to start taking care of her again. It's important to me."

"Then I'll loosen her cinch, and she'll be waiting at the snubbing post."

"Thanks," she said, her smile bright, happiness shining from her emerald green eyes.

Jackson stabled his mount, an old quarter horse named Dakota, after making Glory comfortable for the short wait for her mistress's attention. Then, smiling at how wonderfully the afternoon had gone, he headed for his office. It was his day off, but he was pulling extra duty trying to keep most of the burden of running Laurel Glen off Ross's shoulders while he recuperated and ramped slowly up to full speed.

But when he reached his door Jackson stopped

dead in his tracks. Both Ross and Cole were waiting for him in his office. Ross, who sat on the edge of the desk, looked up from talking to Cole. His cousin sat slouched on the old leather chair across from his desk looking annoyed at best.

"Is there something you want to tell me, Jack?" Ross asked. "Or should I call you Jackson?"

Chapter Twenty

Jackson's heart tripped.

They knew?

And from the look on Ross's and Cole's faces, he'd have to guess, if they did know, the knowledge hadn't come from his mother. He'd come to respect both men and couldn't believe they'd be angry, considering how happy Meg was to have him in her life.

But what if they didn't know and he said the wrong thing?

"Is it a problem for me to use a shortened version of my name?" he asked, carefully. All of a sudden he felt like a GI gingerly negotiating a minefield.

Ross had a steely glint in his eyes as he shifted on the edge of the desk. "Jackson. I know. Jackson Wade Alton, the full name you left off your application, bears a strong resemblance to the name of my sister's late fiancé," Ross added pointedly.

His heart pounded. What should he say? He still

didn't know what they knew about the adoption or if they knew Meg was his mother.

Cole spoke before Jackson could put his foot in it. "It was too much of a coincidence. The way you look so much like Granddad—like all of us, really. And I just can't leave a mystery alone. A cop owed me a favor. He went digging for me. It took a while because of the way records are sealed, but he called me. He tells me my aunt Meg gave up a child for adoption in Colorado. You. So what is it you want, Alton? Half of Laurel Glen? Or just half what it's worth?"

"Cole," Ross said in what sounded like a plea for restraint.

"No, Dad. As a kid I watched you struggle to keep this place alive. You dragged Laurel Glen out of financial ruin twice now, and it almost killed you this last time. I'm not sitting by and watching some Johnny-come-lately show up to cause you or Aunt Meg any heartache."

Jack didn't want this to disintegrate into name calling or erupt into an angry exchange. He took a deep breath and prayed for calm. "Look. Both of you. I didn't come here for any reason but to meet my mother and her family. I never even knew I was adopted until last March. I was furious with my father for keeping me in the dark all those years, and he wasn't too pleased that I intended to find my birth family. So I got a couple of buddies to give me references. I've always worked full time at the Circle A but I've helped them out a time or two when times were tough for them. Everything they said was true, as far as I know. I just didn't want my father trying to manipulate me or talking to any of you.''

"You sound pretty steamed at your father. Were you just as angry at the woman who'd given you away?'' Ross asked.

Jackson shook his head. "Confused by it but not really angry. She left information about Laurel Glen and her engagement ring for me. I found all that with the adoption papers, and it spoke of deep love of her roots and for my father. I found out on the Internet he had died. My mother—my adopted mother—died when I was four, and my father's never gotten over her loss. I felt cheated when I found out I might have had a different life. I wanted to meet my biological mother. That's it. That's all there is to my being here. When I was looking for more information on her and her family, I saw your ad looking for a foreman. You hired me and so I got to meet her that way.''

"If you expect us to believe that, explain to me why all the secrecy?'' Ross demanded.

"Because, brother dear, I asked him to hold off letting anyone know,'' Jackson's mother drawled. She stood in the doorway, arms crossed combatively. "I didn't want to overshadow baby Laurel's birth or our new little Faith's birth, either, with an announcement like this. I thought we'd had enough excitement around here for a while. I didn't see any harm in savoring and building a relationship with Jackson in my own time. I'm overjoyed to have him in my life. I'm proud of the man he is and I'd hoped you would all be happy for me once I told you.''

"Why didn't you tell me before? Years before?" Ross asked. Jackson could hear the hurt that had seeped into Ross's voice.

"That I'll explain in a minute. Right now, however, I think Jack has some explaining to do. To Elizabeth."

Jackson sucked a breath. "Beth?" Had she come back from the house more quickly than he'd anticipated? Had she overheard their accusations?

Meg nodded. "I was on my way down here when I saw her run out of Stable Two. By her movements, I could see she was upset. I called to her and got here as quickly as I could, but she rode toward home on Glory before I could get to her. I assume she overheard the inquisition that was going on in here. She quite possibly has drawn the wrong conclusion. I'm so sorry, son. I never even considered the position I'd put you in by asking for so much time."

I trust you, Jack.

Had Beth said that only an hour ago? Pain exploded in his chest at the thought that he might have lost that trust. He'd been so thankful to see her come so far, and now this situation with his past might send her careening into a prison of her own.

"I had Georgie saddle Dakota for you," Jackson heard his mother say. "Don't just stand there. She was flying over fences as if the devil himself were chasing her. Go. Go!"

Without another second's thought, Jackson started for the door. He heard Cole call his name and turned back.

"I'm sorry," Cole said.

Through his worry for Beth, Jackson heard Cole's regret. "You were only trying to protect your family. Protect my mother. It's a little hard to resent that, but you'd better hope I can square things with Beth."

Cole's nod was a clear acceptance of Jackson's anger. Jackson nodded then swung away. Instantly he saw Georgie silhouetted by the sun and waiting at the stable entrance with Dakota saddled and ready. He ran, galvanized, grabbed the reins, then swung into the saddle in one motion.

How could it all go so wrong? So fast?

But he knew how. Beth wasn't sure of him. And how could she be? She'd known nothing but betrayal in her life and she had to feel he was just like the rest. She was probably off somewhere, crushed and crying.

Elizabeth was so angry she could do nothing but ride hard and fast trying to vent her fury.

He'd lied.

He was no better than her father.

He was out for himself. He'd come to Laurel Glen to hurt the only people besides Maggie and her missing brother she ever loved. Except him.

She'd fallen in love with a sham.

A man whose real name she had not even known. Whose heart she had misread. Whom she never wanted to see again.

She'd just about reached the creek separating her family's land from Laurel Glen when the thunder of hooves close by registered through the cacophony of her angry thoughts.

Jack!

She slapped her heels into Glory's sides, but Jack was the essence of speed in the saddle. Elizabeth found herself plucked from Glory and into Jack's powerful arms in the blink of an eye. Instinctively, she kicked out of the stirrups, hardly believing he'd really try so foolish a trick.

Once she was safely in his lap, she felt Jack's powerful thighs signal the quarter horse to stop. Too angry to care about the danger of the rushing ground, she tried to struggle free. Just as the animal's speed dropped sharply off, Jack slid to the ground and put her away from him.

He put his hands up as if in surrender, but Elizabeth shoved him back a few feet before he could move away. "Are you out of your mind? How dare you even touch me after what you've been up to? You lowlife! Liar! Cheat! Slug!" she went on, feeling powerful in her anger. "You came riding out of the west with your sweet, aw-shucks-ma'am manners and your I-care-about-you-Beth talk and turned my life upside down. And all the time you were a fraud. How dare you! You made me want to live again. You made me believe in dreams again. You showed me a glimpse of a beautiful future then you snatched it away again with your deceit."

"Beth," he said in an odd tone.

The red haze in her mind cleared enough to interpret his hip-shot posture and what looked like laughter in his eyes.

"You slimy worm!" she shouted. "How dare you call me that! How dare you stand there looking so...so...so handsome," she said for want of a better indictment.

She'd thought she'd been angry before, but then Jack went off into peals of laughter. Elizabeth knew with a certainty that if her head had been the top of an anger barometer it would have exploded. Meanwhile Jack wiped his infuriating tears and took several deep, calming breaths. He might be reaching for composure but she felt her blood pounding in her head with even greater force.

Elizabeth didn't even think. It was as if her head had indeed exploded when he reached for her. She stepped toward him, grabbed his wrist as he'd shown her earlier and pointed down toward the muddy stream. In Jack went, twisting at the last moment so he wound up sitting in the shallow murky stream. His ever-present cowboy hat floated in the water next to him.

But did he shout or yell? Oh, no! He grinned.

Grinned!

Speaking slowly to emphasize her anger at having to even ask such a question she demanded, "What is so funny?"

Jack tilted his head, and his grin turned achingly gentle. "You just look so blasted cute, honey. And you've come so far from the prissy, frosty princess I met when I came here. And I have to tell you I love you more than life.''

Elizabeth's anger evaporated in an instant. His declaration muddled her mind and melted her heart. Then she remembered how he'd lied to her. But before the heartbreak could grow worse or her anger could rush to the fore, he went on as if he'd heard her thoughts.

''I didn't want to hold back from telling you why I came here but I didn't want to pressure my mother, either. I figured I was a pretty big shock to her even though she seemed thrilled to meet me. She really seemed to need the time. You seem to have a special place in your heart for Meg. I can't believe you would have wanted me to hurt her in any way.''

''No. Of course I wouldn't. But why didn't you tell me?''

''It wasn't only my secret to tell, Beth. And then there was the problem of her asking questions if I'd told her I was worried about your reaction to being kept in the dark. I was so worried about you and I knew if she got too close to the problem I'd have been tempted to ask her advice. I didn't want to chance betraying your trust, either. Can you find it in your heart to forgive me for handling all this like such a clod?''

How was she to resist such a heartfelt plea? Better yet, seeing the sincerity in his Taggert-blue eyes, why would she want to? Tears fought for release, but she fought just as hard to hold them back. He deserved her strength, not her tears. But when she tried to answer him, her voice failed her. She nodded.

"Thanks," he said. "You know, I've been thinking. You said you'd always wished the Taggerts were your family." He held out his hand. "And if you feel even a quarter of the love for me that I feel for you, I thought maybe you'd consent to be my wife. I come complete with a great mother-in-law for you," he added as if she needed more incentive than a lifetime with the man she loved.

She took his hand, thinking he wanted a hand up to go along with the answer. "I'd be honored," she said, then found herself pulled off balance and into his lap, the muddy stream swirling and splashing around them.

He kissed her—her with her hair dripping muddy water and her clothes a sodden mess.

When he broke the kiss Jack smiled at her and caressed her grimy cheek. "You, Mrs. Jackson Wade Alton to be, are the most beautiful, perfect woman in the world."

And she knew that in his eyes she was. Because he saw past her surface appearance to the person beyond the earthly shell. And more important, she believed it to the core of the soul she'd given to her Lord for cleansing. She was new through Christ Jesus and He had strengthened her. She was Jack's perfect match.

* * * * *

Look for Kate's next book,
the concluding story of Love Inspired's
heartwarming continuity

SAFE HARBOR: *HOME TO SAFE HARBOR*

Available June 2003

Dear Reader,

No one was more surprised than I was when I found
Elizabeth Boyer waiting in line for her own story.
When we met her in the first Laurel Glen book—
The Girl Next Door—she was just a secondary
character who appeared to be a spoiled rich girl.
But my wise editor, Patience Smith, saw something
intriguing and "redeemable" about her, which got
me thinking. As Elizabeth began to take shape, it
was clear that she was misunderstood by many and
needed a special Taggert man to see her as she really
was. But, alas, I'd used them all up!

Then I remembered Aunt Meg Taggert, her early life on
Broadway, her tragic lost-soldier love and her selfless
act of coming home to care for her niece and nephew
even though it meant giving up her acting career. She
left home as a teen, not knowing the Lord, but came
home from New York a believer. What changed her?
And so was born Jackson Wade Alton, the child Meg
gave up for adoption thirty-two years earlier when her
fiancé died, leaving her alone and pregnant.

With his faith a little shaken but still strong, Jackson
arrived on the Laurel Glen scene, looking for his
biological mother. After finding the Lord in her
darkest hour, Meg had picked a Christian family to
raise him, so Jackson was ready to help Elizabeth.
When Jackson met her, sparks flew, but he soon saw
her injured heart and helped her find the Lord, the
Divine healer. Elizabeth felt unworthy until she turned
to the Lord. She learned what so many of us forget—if
God can move mountains, He can heal hearts. And He
will. All we have to do is ask.

God bless,

Kate Welsh